NEWS FROM
BERLIN

Also by Otto de Kat in English translation

A Figure in the Distance (2002)
Man on the Move (2009)
Julia (2011)

NEWS FROM
BERLIN
OTTO DE KAT

Translated from the Dutch by
Ina Rilke

MacLehose Press
New York • London

MacLehose Press
An imprint of Quercus
New York • London

This book was published with the support of The Dutch Foundation for Literature.

N ederlands
N letterenfonds
dutch foundation
for literature

ISBN 978-1-62365-401-6

Library of Congress Control Number: 2015940789

Distributed in the United States and Canada by
Hachette Book Group
1290 Avenue of the Americas
New York, NY 10104

Manufactured in the United States

10 9 8 7 6 5 4 3 2 1

www.quercus.com

For my brother

Chapter 1

Oscar had made the descent from the Lauberhorn to the village so many times that he could have covered the entire distance blindfold. Halfway down, at Hotel Jungfrau, he swerved to a halt, took off his skis and planted them upright in the snow with the poles looped over them. The wooden sun terrace was situated along the hiking trail to Kleine Scheidegg, in full view of the Jungfrau massif, a permanently snow-capped wall to shelter behind in times of peril. Lord Byron himself had visited the hotel at some stage, possibly drawn by the name, and wherever he went tourists would follow. The region was duly discovered: it was here that the English invented winter sports, then churches and hotels made their appearance, as did ski lifts and restaurants. And, typically for the British, a club was founded: D.H.O.—Down Hill Only. That was indeed the direction in which they appeared to be heading: a crumbling empire, a capital city barricaded, colonies under siege.

Oscar sat himself down on a long wooden bench, at a linen-decked table. He gazed out to the other side of the valley. Half past three. The sun was still warm, the summits seeming higher and whiter against a cloudless sky. Eiger, Mönch, Jungfrau, the mountains he knew so well, their names a skipping-song going around in his head. He had lost count of the winters he had been there with Kate and Emma—even last year: quite a feat, considering it was 1940. How they had managed it was something of a mystery. Kate had come over from London, Emma and Carl from Germany, he from Berne. Planes were still flying across a Europe in trepidation, trains were still running, the Swiss welcomed all and sundry. Since the attack on Poland not a shot had been fired, but the sides were drawn and armed to the teeth. All front lines were on red alert. War had been declared, but how to engage, where to start?

In the distance he saw aircraft flying in formation. They moved soundlessly, lost in the blue. The Jungfrau reflected only silence. Every voice was an intrusion, and people spoke in subdued tones, out of reverence for the panorama: an unfathomable expanse of snow, ally of Eternity.

The winter was splendid, but there were few skiers and hikers around. On the terrace were a scattering of Swiss and some Italians. Two tables down from his he noticed a woman on a bench, resting her head against the wall of the hotel. She must have slipped into her seat while he was talking to the waiter. Oscar did not think he had seen her when he was undoing his skis. Was she dozing? She sat motionless, as though she did not belong there. She wore a bonnet of pale gray fur, and a red-and-white checked sweater. He was on the point of averting his eyes—he did not wish to be caught staring—when she took a pair of binoculars from the bag beside her and trained it on the Jungfrau. Oscar couldn't help following her gaze. He saw nothing unusual on the mountain. She peered through the binoculars at length, now and then tucking a strand of hair behind her ear, half under her fur hat. In so doing she gave Oscar a better view of her face. It was not of this world; rather, it was of a higher order of reality. Her teacup remained untouched on the table, nor did he pour his own tea when it came. He wanted to see what she saw. Was she following a climber's ascent to the summit? Had she spotted some rare bird? Was she scanning the slopes for avalanches? She looked upward and he looked with her, then at her again.

The waiter brought him his order of *Rueblitorte*, and he paid the bill. He heard the thud of the hotel door closing, and the next thing he knew she was gone. The teacup was the only trace that she had been there. He cringed inwardly—how absurd to have been so fascinated by her. But her face, that unusual, winsome face.

During the night it snowed unremittingly, as though it would never cease. In the morning, with the snow still pelting down, skiing was out of the question. There was no wind. The few people around in the village had to grope their way ahead; the street lamps were of little help. Oscar had walked down from his hotel to call at his favorite café, diagonally opposite the cog-railway station. Here and there he allowed himself to slide a few paces, with one hand hovering over the wooden fence dividing the road from the long practice slope. His life snowed away from him, he felt both detached and exhilarated, a sense of letting himself go and of bereftness, a fluttery agitation, a devil-may-care wish to forget what he knew and what he had done. He had never known such heavy snowfall. The cog-wheel train would soon remain snowbound in the Lauterbrunnen sidings, leaving the village cut off. Which would suit him just fine. Barricades of snow, yards-high ramparts all around. Nobody going out or coming in. The wider world was a bookish notion, not real, far-off, a phantom, an impossibility. If only he could stay here, in the snow, in the impenetrable nowhere of a hidden village. With each step he sank deeper into the white, in a slow, euphoric haze. Nonetheless, his feet led him unerringly to his café.

It was busier than usual, with most of the tables occupied. Just before shutting the draft door behind him he considered turning back again, into the snow. Right by the entrance there was a table, easily overlooked, which had one vacant chair.

She lowered the newspaper-stick with the broadsheet, behind which she had all but disappeared before, and motioned him to the chair. He recognized her at once, even though he had only seen her in profile.

"Not the kind of weather for binoculars today," he said.

"You ski well for a foreigner."

How did she know he was a foreigner? He noticed that she spoke an old-fashioned, precise sort of German.

"I saw you arrive yesterday, from my window."

So she was staying at Hotel Jungfrau.

She had seen him before he saw her. Insignificant detail, incalculable consequences. The faintest impulse can precipitate an avalanche. She had put her book down, she had taken her binoculars and her sunglasses, she had gone down the corridor, then the stairs, she had asked a waiter to bring her tea. Sunshine. The endless view, the mountains zooming up close in her binoculars. He had been seated to the side, her eyes had not lit on him.

Oscar's thoughts arranged themselves into a semblance of order. Still dazzled by the snow, and by the woman's nearness, he ordered coffee.

"It won't be easy finding your way back to the hotel," he said as she moved to resume reading the newspaper.

"So I realized when I was halfway here," she said calmly, lowering the paper and glancing outside. "But I couldn't stop, I couldn't bear to turn back. A question of narrowed consciousness: all you can do is go forward, your head feels light, you aren't thinking rationally. There's nothing but silence, and the crunch under your boots."

Oscar listened to her voice, not to what she was saying. Heard what had long been forgotten, or repressed. Resonances of something from the distant past, of being carried away, of a girl who took him outside of himself and never delivered him back. Sixteen he had been, and consumed by a wondrous love. He had not told anyone, not even his brother, the brother who was his only friend. Not her either. He would not have known how to tell her he loved her. Love had caused some kind of irreversible shift within him. He had found himself strangely removed from everything that had been perfectly normal only a short time before.

In any case, he would have been incapable of explaining it to her. He had kept her name secret, had never uttered it aloud, for fear of losing her, which had promptly happened. Strange, the way love could also leave you feeling cut off, depleted, making everything meaningless and irrelevant.

The woman regarded him across the table. He saw her eyes for the first time. Only for a second, due to the waiter bringing the coffee and the people squeezing past the back of his chair. Distractions that were not unwelcome. Her eyes were like her voice—challenging. They took him way back, an eternity back, to the ice covering the base of his memory, smooth as glass, and creaking. Treading gingerly on the first ice of the night, over a thinly frozen pond fringed with weeping willows. The girl's embrace, on the way to school. A fleeting interlude of happiness, forged into a short story years later. No, he did not feel challenged, it was different, nothing to do with pressure or being called to account. Her face and her eyes held him fast, he could not have left even if he had wished to.

Beside him there was laughter, the door kept swinging open and shut, snowy overcoats hung all over to drip. Café Eiger was the hub, the haven for those brave enough to venture out of doors. Soup, coffee, hot chocolate, *Schnapps*, cake, good-humored waiters bearing trays. The mood was resolutely festive, no one dreamed of going home. Oscar pointed to the snow falling outside, and asked whether he might order her something else. Yes, he might. The corner they occupied was near invisible to the staff. He took her newspaper and raised it at an angle, stick and all, to attract a waiter's attention. She gave him a quizzical look, because she was also holding the newspaper-stick, and because he seemed utterly unabashed by this. As if they were putting out a flag together. Until he realized that he was signaling the waiter with *her* hand, and quickly let go. The newspaper sank, the flag was furled. Oscar placed the contraption on the table between them, and laughed.

"My apologies for borrowing your hand, the lines of which I'd much rather read than the newspaper, I have to say." He had never, since Kate, paid court to another woman. Now the words came of themselves: carefree, cheerful, free, and with the hopeful echo of a snowbound village high up in the mountains.

"Do you think of yourself as a gypsy? Palmistry is quite an art, you know—let alone reading my palm."

She opened her hand to him. A gesture as though she were shedding her clothes, unafraid of being observed. With utmost care he ran his fingertip along a line across the middle of her palm.

"A life lived to the full, I see. Love, loss, ill health, recovery, and a fresh start," he said in the voice of a fairground fortune-teller.

She closed her eyes a moment, perhaps the better to be aware of the touch of his finger traversing her hand.

"You are an expert, it seems, man-on-the-terrace. I particularly like that bit about a fresh start," she said, all alertness now.

"My dear lady-with-binoculars, my name is Oscar Verschuur. May I know yours?"

She hesitated, he could feel it. Say her name and she was traceable, say her name and she was letting herself go, say her name and it would all begin. Wait, lady-with-binoculars, wait, man-on-the-terrace, why not stop now, why not turn around and go back into the snow while you can, nameless still, unknown, unaccountable, untraceable, for your footprints won't last, the wind will take care of that.

But she did not hesitate for long. Mindful of that fresh start, she told him her name, but not before saying: "Since you know such a lot about me, I expect you know what my name is already."

"As soon as you tell me I'll know if I'm right," Oscar said, in his fortune-teller's tone, draping his scarf over his head like an old crone. It made her laugh.

"Well, Oscar Verschuur, my name is Lara van Oosten."

He blinked. "You're Dutch!" he exclaimed, feigning indignation.

"Yes, afraid so."

Their confidentiality rose as they lapsed, unremarked by either of them, into the informal manner of address.

"But your German is perfect, whereas you knew right away that I'm Dutch by my accent."

Slowly, she nodded.

"Look, here's the waiter, Oscar. You were waving at him with my hand, remember?"

While the snow fell and fell and the windows steamed up, they withdrew into their shell of concentration, deluging one another with questions about their lives as though pressed for time, as though loss loomed. Layer after layer, one question after another, story after story, in a flood of extraordinary candor, albeit that Oscar, true to his programmed discretion, took care to avoid the very least allusion to what he was doing in Berne. After the coffee came the omelet, after the omelet came the coffee, the tea, the cake, the wine, the fading light. At six it finally stopped snowing, and the proprietor announced that the last train to Hotel Jungfrau was leaving in ten minutes. New arrivals stamped the snow off their boots; seldom had the café been more crowded, seldom more packed with promise.

Oscar settled the bill: "I should have bought a day ticket."

Lara stood up: "I'm going walking all day tomorrow."

"In that case, may I come pick you up?"

Again the momentary pause, then agreement and invitation: "Would you?"

Oscar walked her to the station across the road. The platform was already filling up with passengers returning to the hotel. Several people nodded a greeting to Lara. The newspaper kiosk was open; the lights in the shop selling watches were still on. There was not the slightest intimation of the war that was so dangerously close. Oscar did not think of it, neither did Lara. Both were absorbed in the moment of parting, each in a state of weightlessness. The train hummed, men with spades stepped off the tracks, a conductor waved his flag, the driver slammed the door of his engine. Lara raised her eyes, pointing to the bright yellow moon and the starry sky.

"Fine weather tomorrow, Oscar. Forget about being cut off by the snow. We'll all have to go home."

Home? Oscar heard the word, but it had no ring to it. Berne, Berlin, London, he had lost his home long since.

Chapter 2

Kate let herself into her apartment at the quieter end of Barkston Gardens, just off Earls Court Road. She could hear the muffled rumble of traffic on the busy main road, the occasional hoot of a car or a bus, the wail of a fire engine or an ambulance. Kate liked the place. She went through to her balcony and surveyed the communal garden below, to which only the Barkston residents had a key. The noise did not bother her at all. The wider world did not really impinge on her consciousness.

London, late May, 1941. War or no war, the gardener hoed and pruned, the sun shone and birds hopped around in the grass. Kate looked at the buildings across the way: with their gables and roof edging they could have been lifted straight from an Amsterdam canal-side. From her balcony Holland seemed but a small step away, and yet, curiously, she did not miss it. She was aware that she had little thought for the people back home, who had faded into the background of her life as a diplomat's wife. A life that had become splintered in recent years. Oscar at the embassy in Berne, Emma married and living in Berlin, and she working in a London hospital. True, Oscar came over now and then, but she was unhappy about him taking the risk, since the Germans shot at anything airborne. She was pre-occupied more by her work than by Oscar and Emma and her son-in-law Carl. Never before had she known the feeling she now experienced daily: that of being needed. Kate felt mark-edly light and attentive, shaken awake by the war. She was not a nurse—there were plenty of those—her work at the hospital was as a volunteer. Her activities were uncircumscribed and largely unseen, no bandages or blood or thermometers came into it. Mopping a brow here, holding a hand there, tucking in a stray blanket, reading out a letter. Small acts, but of value to the bed-bound.

Kate enjoyed visiting the wards, or the smaller sick rooms with only one or two occupants. She came in from the open air, fresh from the street with a newspaper under her arm, into a world that stood still. The domain of the infirm: a small town of beds crisscrossed by lanes reflecting a hierarchy of diseases and injuries, a laboratory of whispers and groans and tears inter-spersed now and then with a smile or a kind word. An incom-prehensible world of gestures and codes and nameless sorrow, all under the harsh rule of war, the feared and hated war, the specter all endeavored to ignore, in vain.

How the young black soldier managed to make landfall in the Richmond Royal Hospital was unclear. He had been brought over from Africa badly wounded, no one expected him to pull through. But he recovered, little by little. She visited him every day, remaining at his bedside for an hour or so, giving him drink when he was thirsty or plumping his pillows. Small acts, to be sure. The boy responded almost exclusively with his eyes, he hardly spoke. Sometimes he said "Thank you" in an unfa-miliar accent, dusky and warm. More often he dipped his head, or briefly lifted his hand.

Kate knew his name from the medical dossier: Matteous Tunga, soldier in an umpteenth infantry division, wounded en route to Abyssinia. Sucked into the morass of the war, fighting here, fighting there, winning, losing, marching on, nearly drowning, overtaken by storms, caught in a sniper's sights.

Matteous occupied a cubicle on his own—by chance or by design?—and met Kate's eyes the first time she put her head around the door. He lay very still, lifted a few fingers, said nothing, yet all of him cried out for answers. Kate stepped inside, patted the blanket and told him her name. She asked if there was anything she could do for him. No response. She saw the fever in his eyes and hesitated before sitting down on the chair beside his bed. The cramped space, designated for the seriously injured, was more of a storeroom for medical equipment with a bed and a chair squeezed in. Fortunately, there was a window overlooking a courtyard, or rather, there were treetops to be seen and beyond them the wall of another building. The hospital bore a close resemblance to its supply station: the military barracks. Efficient, austere, straightforward. Only the inner courtyard was spared the rigor, having been turned into an English garden with rose beds, apple trees, a long oval beech hedge, jasmine bushes, poppies.

Kate stayed no longer than five minutes the first time. During that short visit she offered him a glass of water and helped him as he drank, her hand cupping the nape of his neck, where the short, bushy hair began. She sensed the fever rising from him, and caught the unusual scent of his skin. She had never been so close to anyone so dark. A wounded man, a black boy thousands of miles from home, a frontline soldier in London, of all places— she would have thrown her arms around him had she dared.

"I'll be back tomorrow," she said. His eyes were closed, but he gave a slow nod of acknowledgment. As Kate was leaving

she noticed the sun slanting across the bed. How black can a
person be, she wondered.

She visited him day after day, week after week, for months on
end. His small room became a second home to her, with each
hour-long encounter an exercise in taciturnity, an exchange of
silences. After a time she could feel that he looked forward to
her visits, and that he relaxed the moment he saw her.

"Matteous," she murmured, and at once he turned his
head on the pillow to face her. A clear-eyed, gentle look, less
fevered than before. He smiled, extended a hand, which Kate
clasped, and they continued to hold hands for a while. He even
chuckled a little, as though rediscovering the ability to laugh.
She let go of his hand, for fear of embarrassing him. She was
determined not to mother him too much, though all her old
instincts were coming to the surface. Once a mother and that
was it: you were lost for the rest of your life, or enslaved, or
whatever you liked to call what motherhood did to women.
Beneath the surface lies a reservoir of talent for loving, according to some doctor Kate had met. That may be, she thought,
but having to carry a reservoir around sounded rather burden-
some. Doubtless a man's idea. A son's. And a rather technical
way of putting it, too. Talent, reservoir, an odd choice of words
for something as elusive and inexplicable as love.

Kate usually said "Matteous" more than once—she so liked
the sound of his name. His reaction was to bring his fist to his
chest, on the side of his heart. A quick, fluid gesture, much as a
Roman Catholic makes the sign of the cross.

Growing accustomed to his garbled English and French, she
came to understand him better. The words began to flow, gradually becoming sentences. And so, after weeks of little more
than gesticulations and looks, they were able to carry on a
conversation. Matteous talked, and she listened to his gravelly,

cautious voice seeking to temper the horrors he related. It was hard for him to get his account in the proper order. His battalion was from the Congo, conscripted by the Belgian governor of the colony. Matteous himself was Congolese, age twenty-three or thereabouts. The village he grew up in was little more than a scattering of huts, the surrounding forest had been his teacher. They were supposed to drive the Italians out of Abyssinia, and set out from Léopoldville northward to Sudan, and on from there. From the fragments of Matteous's story Kate was able to piece together the route taken by his division, not that it really mattered in which direction they had been heading, and whether on foot or in vehicles. She did not need to know exactly where they did battle or where they encamped. She did not ask, and what he told her was sketchy. His journey from Africa to England came out as planes with mattresses on the ribbed steel deck, agonies of pain, bumping along on stretchers, manhandled into the backs of trucks, men in uniform abandoning him in the blistering sun to await onward transportation.

"They can bear that," one of them had said. They, the others, the blacks, they didn't mind a bit of sun. In his feverish brain the remark had taken root.

He had saved the life of a Belgian officer, and had suffered major injuries in the process. The officer insisted on his being taken to London come what may, to save his life in turn. He did not know the name of the officer or what had become of him, but in the meantime here he was, stuck in this hospital for an eternity, and he was desperate to get out, go back, where to he did not know. Kate listened to him and promised to return the following day.

For several days that followed Matteous rambled on, each time beginning his journey from Léopoldville afresh, along the endless River Congo and onward to Abyssinia to throw out the Italian, whoever that might be. The river was a thousand miles long, she discovered.

"Snipers, Miss Kate, snipers in the trees." They had fired at the officer from an ambush; where this had taken place he could not recall. He had managed to drag the officer away in the nick of time, and in so doing ended up with a bullet in the back and another in his foot. The odd thing was that he had been able to carry on walking for a further hundred yards; he had felt the impact of the bullets, but no pain.

Matteous spoke in simple words, with long pauses. Sometimes he dozed off, and she would leave without rousing him. Rain against the window, stormy skies, sunshine, March, April, May, from winter to spring: the boy was on the mend, watched over by Kate. Miss Kate, who helped him move into the main ward once he had sufficiently recovered.

Leaning over her balcony, Kate reflected on Matteous. He would be discharged from the Richmond in two days' time, but where was he to go?

Her mind returned to the single occasion he had told her of a different experience, more harrowing than that of war. How, a long time ago, his village was attacked, how his father was axed to death, and his mother dragged away. How he had fled into the forest. Matteous had wept soundlessly, clutching Kate's arm with a shaking hand—not for long, just a few halting sentences. He had not spoken of it again.

London had been under bombardment for months, with German aircraft flying over the city center at the most unexpected times. During the previous fortnight, however, all had been quiet. The air-raid sirens had fallen silent—almost eerily silent, for her mind was programmed to hear them. Barkston

Gardens had been spared until now. Her neighborhood apparently held little appeal: no factories, no government offices, no harbor, no prominent buildings. It was like living in a village. One or two pubs and restaurants, some shops, a school, small gardens, a pharmacy, a church. Children played in the street—how wonderful, playing in the eye of the storm, how superior of them! The only incursions on normality were the air-raid sirens. And the mandatory blackout.

Should she offer to put him up at her apartment? Her heart said yes, but her head said no. Matteous would quite likely be returning to the Congo, although she could not imagine what sort of life awaited him there. The daily hour in his company, the wary rapprochement and the struggle to find words, the sounds of the ward and the intermittent voices and laughter from the courtyard, all these things gave her an unprecedented sense of kinship with a stranger. She could not speak to Oscar or Emma about this, nor did she wish to: they would not understand. Oscar and Emma lived in a different world.

She would find lodgings for him in the neighborhood, not too close and not too far.

A black beacon in a surf of beds. She saw him at once when she entered the vast ward, which for the past weeks had served as his bivouac. It was indeed a bivouac, a foxhole into which he had dug himself. But today Matteous was up and dressed in an old, shabby uniform. Hardly anyone spoke, and he kept quiet himself. A few nurses were attending to him; their manner was brisk, though not without kindness. He stared at them as though they were apparitions drifting by. Clouds over a battlefield.

Kate stood in the doorway, waving to him. He took a step forward, stiffly like an old man. The men lying in the beds on either side nodded toward him as he came past, one raised a hand in greeting, all in silence. A salute to a soldier, a solo parade reviewed by a small army of patients brought in from all over, bandaged and splinted and patched up. Matteous, soldier, made his way across Africa and was never the same again. Now he made his way across the ward, to the door where Kate stood waiting. She took his luggage: a wicker basket. A basket with a lid. He turned around one last time with a shy, near-rueful glance, as though taking flight from an enemy that had already been defeated. He raised his hand to an imaginary cap, and went through the door which Kate held open for him.

On their way to the exit they paused in the courtyard overlooked by his cubicle, from where he used to hear the nurses' voices. He smelled the jasmine Kate had told him about, the hedges and the flowers: fragrances of a foreign continent.

She led him gently past the garden, through the reception hall, to the street outside. They went to catch the bus Kate always took to the city center. Matteous seemed half asleep, she thought, or rather, as if he were dreaming. His movements were unsure, everything about him seemed dumbfounded. She realized that London was unlike anything he had ever before seen. And that the ease with which she walked down the street with him was unsettling.

Kate had found him a studio on Earls Court Road, ten minutes away from her apartment. She had not yet told Matteous about this, and was unsure about his reaction. She explained when they were sitting side by side in the bus. Did he understand, did he know what she meant? He stared motionless out of the window, incredulity in his eyes at the city he found himself in. He had spoken of Élisabethville a few times, but to her it had sounded more like a sprawling village.

She sensed his bewilderment, and repeated her news about the room she had rented for him. He replied with a quick fist to his heart, and gazed out of the window again. The route traveled by the bus was not exactly cheering. At the Richmond Royal Hospital all was clear-cut and regulated, but outside all was devastation. The whole bus route was a miracle, as Kate reminded herself daily. Despite the danger and disruption, London Transport kept daily life moving. Buses had to run, and they did. Stops might be bombed beyond recognition, depots shattered, roads impassable, but somewhere, in some magician's den, new routes were contrived, new bus stops organized, broken vehicles replaced.

As they drew nearer to the city center the traffic thickened, and Matteous stopped looking outside. He said something Kate did not understand. Perhaps he was not addressing her, for it was more of an invocation, or a short prayer in a language she did not recognize, the language of his parents. The other passengers stared at them, and especially at him. A bird of paradise from overseas, a soldier with a wicker suitcase, a displaced person. Kate helped him down from the bus; his wounded foot was not yet properly healed. Following him up the stairs to his room she could see how poorly it functioned, whereas out on the street he had been able to hide his limp. Well, at least they wouldn't be wanting him back in the army for the foreseeable future, she told herself.

The room with a bed and a kitchen in the corner was not much bigger than his cubicle at the hospital. Matteous left his luggage on the bed and walked to the window. Kate followed him with her eyes, hearing the soft hiss of a gas geyser at her back. His shoulders, the window, the traffic, the worn carpet on the floor, the melancholy of it all. They had come a long way.

She from a life among clever diplomats and well-educated folk, he from the raw Congo heartlands.

"Why?" he said.

Now it was Kate who failed to respond. It was a question she was unable to answer. Why had she taken the trouble all these months to visit him daily, to listen to him, fetch him when he was discharged, find him lodgings? Of all the soldiers she had offered assistance to in the hospital, Matteous was the only one to have affected her so deeply. A dreamed-of son, someone who needed her, a lost child, a boy holding out his hand? There was no explanation, she thought, and anyway she did not need one. Looking past Matteous out of the window, Kate saw that it had begun to rain, and his question dissolved in the patter on the glass.

Chapter 3

Oscar wore a dark-gray coat, a dark-gray hat and dark-gray pants, beneath which his tan shoes struck a jarring note.

He walked hurriedly under the arches of the Gerechtigkeitsgasse. Seven p.m., the city was all but deserted. Sunshine had been predicted, but it was raining, and the tourists, such as there were, stayed away. Oscar heard the echo of his footsteps: a pleasing sound, breaking his own small sound barrier. Reflecting on this, he slowed his pace, his haste receding. The shop windows slid past him. He paid no heed, he saw nothing and no one.

Oscar Verschuur, age fifty-six, was on his way to the first secretary of the Swedish legation. It was the second day of June 1941, and it was raining in Berne, capital of sun and snow and flower-filled Alpine meadows. Welcome to the heart of Europe, welcome to an oasis of tranquility and rectitude. *Willkommen!* The word was blazoned on placards and windows—God, how the sound of German had come to grate on his ears.

He knew who else would be present. David Kelly, the British resident minister. Pinto, the Portuguese military attaché. Horst Feller, a Swiss diplomat. Walter Irving, the American chargé d'affaires. Ismet Fahri, the Turkish envoy. And the American journalist Howard Smith, just arrived from Berlin. It was to be an informal dinner party, all protocol having been waived. Ambassadors mixing with lower-ranking diplomats was generally frowned on, and having a journalist present always carried an element of risk. And risk-taking was not normal ambassadorial practice, but in Berne, on that particular day in June, other considerations applied. Over the past weeks of gathering menace in a world already in the grip of fear, everything had come to be viewed in a new light.

Verschuur had recently learned the date. It was quite soon: June 22, just under three weeks from now. But he knew he had to keep the information to himself, there was no other option. He was a past master at keeping secrets, it had become second nature to him. He enjoyed it, it was food and drink to him. It was what he did for a living, his brief being to uncover what lay hidden, and to cover up such tracks as had been inadvertently exposed. He was a cover-up artist. A diplomat, on secondment to the Dutch legation, with a covert mission.

But this secret was different. In an unguarded moment, he had been hurled out of his orbit by a message to which he could not shut his ears, even as his lips had to remain sealed. The ramifications were immeasurably vast and terrifying. Three more weeks to go, and it was impossible to breathe a word. Yet there was every reason to give out warnings, call government ministers, sound the alarm, raise a great hue and cry.

Oscar crossed to the other side of the Junkerngasse, then turned into the Kreuzgasse; he walked past the cathedral and down the Schifflaube, stopping at no. 52. The door was opened by a maid, who took his coat and hat. He was late, too late according to the rules of diplomacy, the higher ranks having already arrived. But there were to be no rules this evening, no one was there in an official capacity, it had more the air of a conspiracy. Verschuur was acutely aware of the anomaly of the scene before him: a British ambassador and a Swiss diplomat having a chat at a side table over a carafe of white wine, a Turkish envoy resting his hand on the shoulder of an American, a Swede showing a German newspaper to a Portuguese. The diffusely lit reception room was the stage for a shadow play in which he, Verschuur, was the last actor to make his entrance. Unheard music passed through his mind, the voices, the gestures all around him, an entire alphabet of goings-on. He noted that they all raised their heads when he came in, saw a smile here, a wave of the hand there. Björn Henderson, the Swedish host, stepped forward to greet him: *välkomna*, welcome, *willkommen*. That German word again.

Henderson pointed to Oscar's shoes.

"Just as well the boss has gone off to the mountains, Oscar." Sweden's neutrality was not to be compromised, least of all by a man's footwear. "That color would have had him putting on his sunglasses and turning the lights down—good grief."

"I knew he'd be away, Björn, or I'd have worn my funeral shoes." Which would have suited his mood rather better, he thought to himself.

Henderson and he were on good terms, they were the same age, and both had a stubborn streak to their character. Not for them the likes of ambassadorial or high office. Oscar harbored no resentment about this, the very idea of such a post was distasteful to him—having to attend tedious dinner parties and useless formal audiences in a straitjacket of directives and unattainable proposals, what could be worse? Still, there were several astute, upstanding men among the diplomats of his acquaintance.

Wherever he went, Oscar found ways of circumventing the Foreign Ministry's rules. Or of breaking them, laughing them off. He was not supposed to consort with ambassadors and ministers more than was strictly necessary, but for reasons unknown, objections had never been raised to his presence among them, nor for that matter to his lower, or at any rate unclear, status. He had more or less conquered his own position, no one knew quite how or when, but at a certain moment it was a fact. He was a diplomatic freewheeler, dispatched on far-flung assignments that were considered too delicate or challenging for ordinary civil servants. A diplomat with a special mission, an attaché, someone in possession of a *laissez-passer*. He knew everybody, but very few people knew him. His card said: Dr. O.M. Verschuur, Foreign Affairs, Kingdom of the Netherlands. That was all. Oscar Martinus Verschuur had earned his doctorate, *summa cum laude*, with a thesis on the Anglo-Zulu War in South Africa, paying particular attention to the battles of Isandlwana and Rorke's Drift on January 22, 1879. Unusual subject matter, brilliant analysis as well as presentation. A touch eccentric, a touch unconventional in the context of contemporary historical studies. He had done field research, seeking out the elderly survivors of the battle to hear their descriptions firsthand, and the resulting work, written in English, had the makings of a full-blown novel. His argument was that the defeat at Isandlwana marked the beginning of the end of the British Empire. "Here they come, as thick as grass and as black as thunder," a British soldier had cried. It was a warning quoted by Verschuur during the public defense of his thesis, in response to which the audience froze. Kate had been watching him from the front row, her expression grave and tense.

Now he saw them all around him: German armies, as thick as grass and as black as thunder. Black and tightly packed, more than ever girded up for the inferno, waiting for Zero Hour.

"Operation Barbarossa, Papa, June 22nd, they're going to invade Russia, Carl saw the order," Emma had hissed at him, her face tight with shock and distress. "They're going to invade Russia, Carl says it's definite!"

Carl Regendorf, his son-in-law, was employed at the Foreign Ministry in Berlin, the only place where some elements of resistance against Hitler and Ribbentrop lingered.

Oscar had been with the Dutch legation in Berlin for a spell during the Thirties. Kate and he lived in Fasanenstrasse. The happiest years of their marriage, in the midst of a rising tide of violence and betrayal. Emma had met Carl at a dinner party at their house. Oscar had seen it all unfold that evening. Kate had been very concerned, but Emma and Carl were living life to the full, in perfect harmony. In the tumult of Berlin.

It was five days since Emma and Carl unexpectedly found themselves in Geneva: a tour of duty with Carl's boss, Adam Trott. A special mission, during which Emma was permitted to accompany her husband as his secretary, a ploy they had used successfully before. Emma had called her father from the hotel, and Oscar had taken the first train from Berne to meet them. They had been discreet, he thought, but was that true? Switzerland was rife with German spies, more so than any other country. It was in the restaurant, when Carl absented himself from the table for a moment, that she told him. Barbarossa. So that's what they called it, the barbarians.

They had fallen silent when Carl reappeared, after which Emma made some remark about her mother. But her words kept pounding in his brain.

The train back to Berne took him past Nyon, Rolle, Morges, Lausanne. He noted the names of the stations, each one a small paradise, and was struck by the baffling ordinariness of everyday life as seen from his carriage window. Riding on a Swiss train often reminded him of being ill in bed as a child, listening to the reassuring street noises—the rag-and-bone man's cry, the garbage man ringing his bell—and feeling soothed and snug. Not today, though. On this train, passing through innocent stations along the lake, with hayfields creeping up the mountainsides and sailing boats on the mirror of water, Emma's whispered message weighed like a stone on his heart. The content defied the imagination, while the fact that he knew became ever more terrifying. The long-expected attack on Russia was finally to be launched. And he knew the date and the hour.

Operation Barbarossa, a code name for murder, obviously, even as it was a childish appeal to old myths and legendary heroes. Super-kitsch, if it weren't for the deadly intent. Emma had been incapable of keeping the news to herself. She had blurted it out to her father, who she was sure would know what to do. The fear in her tone had been unmistakable, as well as the urgent, unvoiced appeal for action.

At the station of Lausanne he had got off, feeling choked by the stuffiness of his compartment, and even more by the turmoil in his mind. He had no appointments in Berne that evening, so there was plenty of time for a stroll by the lake. Trees and bushes were heavy with blossom on this late afternoon of May 28, in the second year of the war. The boulevard was agreeably alive with strolling couples, cyclists, sailors, tourists. Oscar wandered off in the direction of the music he could hear in the distance. It came from the terrace of Hôtel Beau Rivage, where a small orchestra was playing English tunes—emphatically English, he thought. A few tables were still vacant. He sat down, ordered a glass of Dôle, and waited. Spring on the shore of Lake Geneva. As though time stretched out into forever.

He watched the gulls flying in wide arcs over the water. Where on earth did all those birds come from? They belonged by the sea, surely. He remembered standing at the window as a boy and throwing out crusts of bread for the gulls to catch, which they did with ease, somersaulting through the air, watching him with their orange beady eyes.

And so Oscar sat, wrapped up in his thoughts, at a neatly laid table not far from the band: violinists in dinner jackets, pianist in evening dress, trombone player in red. Uniforms of peace, clownish outfits of neutrality. He picked up a newspaper left behind on a nearby table. *Die Nation*, extra edition. "BISMARCK SUNK" was the headline splashed across the entire front page, with further down, in much smaller font: "Crete All But Lost." News from the front: filed by a reporter, typeset by a compositor, delivered by a paperboy, only to be discarded on a white tablecloth beside an empty wine glass on a summer's evening. Texts such as these circled the globe, and were read without their portent being properly understood by anyone. A banner of blank letters, bloodless, hollow: *Bismarck* destroyed, Crete all but lost. Oscar read the paper; he knew what it said, but felt nothing. Everything going on simultaneously, all the things happening around him, it was all too much to grasp. Man's imperviousness to what was going on outside his field of vision was extraordinary. He traced a pattern of lines on the tablecloth with his fork, stared at the newspaper, laid the fork down, signaled a waiter and asked for the menu.

"This morning shortly after daybreak, the *Bismarck*, virtually immobilized, without support, was attacked by British battleships that pursued her," Churchill was quoted as announcing to the House of Commons. "And I have just received news that the *Bismarck* has sunk." Applause. Hear, hear. Shortly after daybreak, Oscar mused. The bleak morning sky over a stormy

sea. And then sinking, sinking to the bottom fast. Ears and
eyes aflame, throats parched in terror and rage. How did such
a calamity proceed, he wondered. The newspaper provided no
answer, all was rumor and speculation. There were reports of
hand-to-hand fighting in Crete, meaning the fixed bayonet, pistol in hand, grenade-packed belt, possibly even a knife between
the teeth. Fighting and falling. Blown to bits, mown down, lost
and destroyed. Headlines for polite discussion over a lakeside
dinner. Shortly after dusk. Music.

Despondency crept up on him as he realized yet again how
relentlessly things took their course, how simultaneously and
obscurely, and how the significance kept eluding him of so
many contradictory events taking place just a stone's throw
away. Nevertheless, he appeared unmoved as he pored over
Die Nation, the only Swiss newspaper to persist in its anti-Nazi
stance. On the whole the press took a back seat, leaning a little
this way, then that. Dillydallying. Nothing new about human
misery, sir, we have to put our foot down, we're being inun-
dated by refugees and it can't go on; watch out, folks, let's not
rub our bad-tempered neighbor the wrong way; careful now,
steady on. The hirelings of the press were forever glancing over
their shoulders, unless holed up in their bunkers of shrewd
impartiality. The journalists of *Die Nation* were the exception.
Oscar had great respect for the editor, whom he had met in
Berne. A driven man, who despised most of his fellow Swiss.
He had visited the border crossings, had seen Jews being turned
away without mercy. Anyone having witnessed that would
never again rest easy, he had said. Murder at one remove: Death
in a Swiss customs officer's cap. His newspaper stood alone in
daring to attack the government. Oscar did not always see eye
to eye with the editor, although he too was critical of Swiss
politics on various counts. In spite of the border restrictions,

however, people still managed to get into the country. Oscar knew this; he worked closely with the people who smuggled them in, he knew the routes, the dangers, and the courage of certain Swiss men and women. On many a moonless night he had stood waiting for a small group to come over from France. Often in vain. Waiting was hardly a heroic activity, but each time just a few of them made it over the border it felt like a major victory.

His ruminations came to an abrupt halt. Something had stirred in the periphery of his vision. Then he recognized him. It was the way the man was lighting his cigarette, his head bent low as though scanning the ground at his feet. The same gesture had struck him at the restaurant in Geneva, during his lunch with Emma and Carl. He had been unaware of the man with the newspaper until that curious ducking of the head to light a cigarette. And so here he was again, on the far side of the terrace, engrossed in a magazine, a man like any other taking a rest after a stroll.

Oscar was unperturbed. Being followed was a frequent occurrence, he was used to it. At first he had found it intimidating and irksome, but in due course he was able to tell quite quickly whether or not someone was watching him. In Geneva, though, he was taken by surprise, engrossed as he was in the anticipation of seeing Emma and Carl again. He had promised himself he would provide Kate with a detailed description of how they looked, what they said, and how they were managing in Berlin. But as things stood, a letter was probably not an option. Oscar glanced at the shadow-man and considered actually beckoning him. Often an effective way of making the person back off in confusion. Could the word "Barbarossa" have been overheard? There had not been many people in the restaurant, and the sneak had been sitting at the next table. But no, Emma had spoken softly and rapidly, or rather, she had whispered. Whispering was suspicious, obviously, even if the man had been out of earshot. It would merit a brief report: *O.V. with daughter in G. Whispered exchange in absence of C.B. Followed to L. then lost contact. 28.5.41.* He would shake the man off, no trouble at all. He was trained in vanishing. This time he would fall back on the tried and trusted method of putting his hat and empty briefcase on the table, asking the waiter for the men's room, going into the hotel, settling his bill there, and then making his exit by the back door. The Beau Rivage hotel had several back doors, so making a getaway without being spotted was not a problem. Not that it was necessary, beating a retreat, but he wanted to take some positive action. His vexation about the German watcher was greater than usual. He tried once more to recall exactly how clear Emma's voice had sounded. Barbarossa. Although they had been speaking Dutch, that word could have been picked up by a German, any German. Especially a German. Barbarossa, what did that name remind him of? A medieval ruler, a tyrant of old, something Germanic, something from a revered past, something Hitlerian. Oscar's brain, well-versed in history, took no time in coming up with the answer: the German emperor leading the crusades, twelfth century or thereabouts. That was the underlying idea, of course, it was all about a crusading ruler with endorsement from on high.

Oscar vacillated. Should he go or should he stay? Stay, there was no hurry. Take a long look at the menu, call the waiter, give him your order, ask for more wine, turn the pages of your newspaper at leisure. All of which he proceeded to do. The man sitting some yards away was as nothing to him, a mere smudge at the corner of his gaze. The marina facing the hotel was crowded with sailing craft and rowing boats. Children ran up and down the long wooden jetties. It was eight o'clock, evening fell as the darkness rose up in layers from the lake. The mountains on the far side melted slowly but surely from view.

The newspaper lay untouched on his lap as Barbarossa receded from his consciousness. His thoughts turned to her, and where she might be.

Chapter 4

She caught the hum of aircraft. English? Emma waited for the air-raid sirens to go off. They did not. Presumably Luftwaffe. Everyone was tense after the heavy bombing of the city a fortnight ago. Dahlem had not been hit, a pity in a way, as Himmler and Ribbentrop lived virtually around the corner. But the English obviously did not know that. Berlin-Dahlem, little more than a village until quite recently, had been quietly amalgamated into the city. The streets still smelled of earth and meadows, there was a church, a farmers' market, there were gardens and old country houses. The U-Bahn had a terminal there, where Carl took the train to the Foreign Ministry every morning at seven.

Foreign affairs were becoming less foreign by the day, what with all the new German conquests, Emma remarked drily. They would be making themselves redundant next.

Carl had to smile at her laconic, un-German sense of humor, her plain speaking. Quick, fearless, and unwaveringly good-tempered she was. Like him. They were two of a kind, high-level poker players, leading intense lives on the edge of danger. Carl worked for Adam von Trott, the all-knowing, unflappable

Trott, who knew everybody who mattered, who swept his associates along with him in his convictions. And his convictions were diametrically opposed to those of his superiors and the almighty superior in whose name all was directed and done.

They had just returned from Switzerland, their travel bags were still in the hall. It was Monday morning, June 2. They had taken the overnight train, and Carl had gone straight from the station to his office. Emma was exhausted; traveling by sleeper did not agree with her. She wondered what had been the matter with her father. She had never seen him so distracted, so utterly wrapped up in his own thoughts, like a mathematician brooding over a problem, and it had taken some effort to get his attention at all. But the news about Barbarossa had shaken him awake. On reflection, she couldn't see how she could have been so reckless as to burden him with that secret. It had been going around and around in her head for days, she hadn't known which way to turn. Her father might be able to do something—who else? The effect had been galvanizing. Her distracted father, sitting opposite her in a world of his own, had come crashing back to earth on the instant. He darted a glance around him and asked in a low, urgent voice: "Are you quite sure about this?" She only had time to say yes when Carl reappeared, and quickly changed the subject: "What about Mama, when will you be seeing her again?"

She had kept putting it off, but at some point she would have to confess that she had told her father. She prayed that Carl would understand. In the meantime her poor father would be beside himself with worry. What would he do with her information?

Ever since Carl came home with the news they had been in a welter of conflicting emotions. Carl had even raised a little cheer, despite the gravity. It would mean the downfall of the

Nazis, the end of Hitler. The Russians were unbeatable, any invading army would be swallowed up by the sheer vastness. Adam was of the same opinion. Carl was his chief assistant, his junior by only a few years, intelligent, disciplined, sharp. Trott, however, was sharper, he could argue anyone into a corner. A man of many talents. Carl did not hide his esteem for Trott. Emma sometimes felt obliged to temper his enthusiasm, although she too admired the man for his intellect as well as his disarming powers of persuasion. They had accompanied him to Switzerland, which created a splendid opportunity for Emma to meet her father. Carl and he made regular trips to neutral countries, traveling even as far as Russia and America on diplomatic visits to embassies and conferences, their aim being to foster links with the enemy, their secret ally. Emma was many times alone. They had no children, having decided to postpone starting a family until the war was over. And that did not seem likely for the foreseeable future.

Carl's news was deeply distressing: Germany planning to invade Russia on June 22, the whole world taken over, all hell let loose. The ministries were abuzz with "Russia, Russia." Trott was agitated in the extreme, for all that he never doubted the gangsters would lose in the end. He set up meetings, made efforts to speak with generals, visited friends all over the country. With Carl in his wake as his adviser. Was there any way of stopping the insanity? How many people would have to die first?

Emma went out into the garden, telling herself the bags could wait. Her father's odd behavior preoccupied her thoughts. It was not at all like him to be so remote, so timid almost. He had snapped back to his usual self the moment she told him, though. But his evasiveness rankled: she had been so looking forward to seeing him after more than a year's separation. He had hugged her with a strange sort of detachment, shyly, like a boy. And it was quite soon after she blurted the news that he got up and left, saying a hurried goodbye. Her father was not the most accessible of parents at the best of times, but this was different. She tried to think of an explanation, but the mystery remained.

Rhododendrons in bud, lilies of the valley, an old mulberry tree, hedges in blossom—Emma was surrounded by spring. These were the fragrances of her grandmother's garden in Hengelo, with the Great War just over the border. Her own garden in Dahlem smelled just the same—fragrances that telescoped time.

Their house stood in a web of green lanes. There was no wind, and all was tranquil. From close by came the reassuring sound of a hedge being clipped, while next door's dog dug a hole in the gravel with audible enthusiasm. Germany was mobilized to its furthest corners, but standing here you would never have thought it.

She heard a car approaching, faster than normal, then the belligerent slam of car doors half a minute later. Two unremarkable men in long coats—even in fine weather they wore coats, apparently, with the collars turned up. So this was what the Gestapo looked like. It was her first thought when they pushed the gate open and entered the garden without saying a word. Facing them, Emma's expression was not so much questioning as mildly ironic.

"They took me to Prinz-Albrecht-Strasse, Carl. I was there. They let me go after a few hours. They wanted to know—they knew all along of course—whether the man we'd met in Geneva was my father. And what I was whispering about."

Prinz-Albrecht-Strasse 8, secret police headquarters, watchtower of hell, rumored to be a place where more people went in than came out. However, Emma had not been held for very long, presumably to avoid complications with the Foreign Ministry, although Prinz-Albrecht-Strasse bowed to no one. A pin-prick against Trott? A little dig at them, to show that they were being watched, wherever they were? The mere fact that she was Dutch cast suspicion on Emma, she was given to understand, and having a father working at the Dutch legation in Switzerland was enough reason to be sent to a camp. Hints, intimations of punishable offenses, the staple ingredients of the murder-by-stealth methods favored by the clerks of Himmler's elite corps.

"What was that about you whispering something?"

Her explanation shook her husband more than she had foreseen.

"My God, Emma, how could you? I told you in confidence!"

"I couldn't help it, all I could think of was what you'd said, Carl. And he was so . . . it was as if he were worlds away, almost a stranger. I wanted him to know what we know. Only three more weeks. And so I told him, and he was back with his feet on the ground straightaway. I hope he'll do something with it. He must."

Carl said nothing. The warning they had received today was impossible to take lightly. Emma's arrest, albeit brief, was a threat of the most direct sort. Thank God they had not over-heard what she relayed to her father in Switzerland, or he would never have seen her again. This was the opening gambit in a chess game, with the Gestapo making all the moves. Carl Regendorf, we're hot on your trail, and your trail leads to von Trott, that boss of yours. We don't like your boss very much, nor his friends and associates. We don't like anything about you, really, not your wives, your children, or your families. Arrogant intellectuals, the bunch of you, with your nice houses and fancy talk and names and your manicured notions and unreadable books and your foreign connections. It's high time for change, you see, and so we'll get things going by arresting one of your women. Give her a scare, show how much we know about her. Everything, in fact. Just a little bit of fun on our part, as you will appreciate. We all have to start somewhere.

Prinz-Albrecht-Strasse dungeons, no better place for comedy.

Carl and Emma sat in the conservatory in the fading light, their bags still unpacked. Emma had called him to ask if he could come home early. She was upset, but not by any means panic-stricken.

"And as I was leaving, one of them grinned at me and said: 'By the way, your mother's quite a looker.' I wonder what he was getting at. Mama has only been in Switzerland once since the outbreak of war. Do you suppose they have suspicions about her as well?"

Carl made no reply, his mind being filled with Emma's arrest and the repercussions that might have for Trott. In hindsight, of course, making contact with her father had been very foolish. But it had seemed such a shame not to take the opportunity of seeing him briefly. Just to be among themselves, no treading on eggshells for a change. He often wondered what exactly Emma's father was doing in Switzerland. A solitary job, apparently, not that he seemed lonely. The lakeside restaurant had not been particularly busy, Carl reflected. Only three or four occupied tables, one of which was next to theirs. A man had been sitting there reading a newspaper with screaming headlines: the *Bismarck* had been sunk the previous day. The beginning of the end—he clearly remembered the thought entering his mind. The beginning of the end, a pleasing notion—as if you could look in the future. From now on it was the British ruling the waves—that was what the sinking of the *Bismarck* meant. And they were gaining the upper hand in the sky, too. They flew over Germany every day.

And then to go and invade Russia—how brainless could you be? The beginning of the end, which would come in six months, he thought. At most a year and it would all be over. On the other hand, one couldn't be sure. Huge armies had been formed—Trott knew the exact numbers—half the country was in uniform. The call of the Fatherland had been heard, and the answer was marching in the streets. Anyone voicing the wrong views was strung up with piano wire. Oh yes, there was music in execution, or imprisonment, or strangulation, or plain clubbing to death. That man with the newspaper, could he have been spying on his father-in-law? Likely enough, come to think of it. How careless of them to talk so freely. Just as well the tables were set fairly wide apart. The more expensive the food the more space there was between one party of diners and the next. Businessmen could not tolerate tables having ears. Nor could politicians. Perhaps that was why his father-in-law had picked that smartish restaurant.

Emma had mentioned something about her mother, which puzzled him. A looker? Her mother, quite a looker? Not like the Gestapo to pay compliments, why would they. She was blonde, though, which the Nazis favored, perhaps that was what they were getting at. It was all very strange.

Blackout time. Carl pulled the curtains across the windows, which were papered over in black, but he stepped outside anyway to make sure not a chink of light was to be seen. Inspection was being tightened all the time, and the consequences of infringement were accordingly dire. Trott had told him a joke someone had made about seeing the light shining in a town house window: "That group must have signed a private peace treaty with the Allies." Peace, a word of fairytale resonance.

When Emma and Carl first met it was still peacetime, but only just. Spring 1938, in Fasanenstrasse, a treelined side street off Kurfürstendamm. The Verschuurs had been recalled to the Netherlands, and were giving a round of farewell dinner parties.

Carl had already met Oscar Verschuur, having supplied him with intelligence on various occasions in the past. He had accepted the invitation with pleasure. He was the youngest person there, with one exception: Emma, his table companion for the evening. She would be his companion for life, too, although at the time he felt that the circumstances were not in his favor. That night, there had been no past and no future, only her presence beside him. Their exchanges had been mutually pleasing, candor being met with equal candor. Tones of voice, looks, gestures, smiles, and the silences in between, all were in agreement.

Oscar Verschuur had given a speech, thanking everyone for their friendship and support over the years, and had raised a glass to peace, or rather to what was left of it. Which was not very much, given the shameless stoking of the fires of war. Emma and Carl saw nothing and no one. At their end of the dinner table, in the company of Dutch, French, German, Swiss, Portuguese, Swedish and British guests, a very different fire was being fanned. War and peace did not come into it. Emma's German was fluent, better than that of her parents. Coming from her, Carl's language sounded so much more pleasing than what he was used to hearing in public—the barking of commands, the voice of propaganda, the hysterical rants of the Idiot.

Saying goodbye to her, he was seized with doubt whether he had interpreted her behavior toward him correctly. They stood by the cloakroom in the throng of departing guests, all of whom seemed to be shaking hands as though they were parting forever. Emma held his eyes, her expression intense, her hand resting on his arm.

"Will we meet again? Because I'm leaving in a few weeks."

"Tomorrow?"

She smiled, thank God, and said: "Yes, fine."

"Tomorrow" had turned into every day, and then into day and night. They had married before the year was out, as if the Devil himself were nipping at their heels.

Carl stepped inside after his blackout inspection to find Emma standing motionless in the hall, next to the unpacked luggage. When he went up to her he saw that she was crying.

Chapter 5

"Well, Howard, how are things over there nowadays?"

David Kelly, head of the British legation, turned to the journalist fresh from Berlin with the eagerness of a sniffer dog. The round table in Björn Henderson's study was just large enough to seat eight guests, several of whom knew each other quite well from other postings and earlier times. The traveling circus of diplomacy: dinner parties in Ankara, Buenos Aires, Belgrade or Stockholm, in disparate company and disparate settings, yet secure in an unchanging etiquette and a sameness of tone and vocabulary.

Henderson's study gave Oscar the illusion of home. Bookcases on all sides, a walnut desk, a leather armchair, paintings on every available wall space, a small pantry with bottles of drink and glasses. A dark red carpet on the floor, a domed ceiling painted pale yellow, soft lighting on the books, candles, photographs of Stockholm. All was geared to forgiving and forgetting.

"Is your house microphone-free, Henderson?" Howard Smith said brightly, but the undertone was serious.

"You'll have to ask Horst, it's up to the Swiss. But no, Howard, we've searched the place from top to bottom, no bombs."

Smith turned to Kelly: "Your aircraft have been keeping us pretty busy lately, David. I've lost count of the times I had to go down to the shelter, and I've had just about enough if it. Chronic sleep deprivation is the number-one popular ailment. Still, for the past ten days you've been behaving yourselves—a question of fuel rationing? If you could keep away a bit longer, it would be much appreciated. I heard a curious story the other day, about so-called shelter parties, organized by people who have developed a liking for air raids. Nightly air raids foster fellowship. You all are bringing Berliners closer together, literally and figuratively. An interesting side effect. Just think: masses of people huddled together in the middle of the night with snacks and drinks, candlelight and songs, just longing for the sirens to go off. Suffice it to say I am not one of them."

Kelly gave a short laugh. He was keen to hear what Smith had to say for himself in this company. Oscar knew the journalist from his days in Berlin: an American C.B.S. correspondent, and the sharpest analyst of Nazism around. Through Emma and Carl, Oscar was well aware of how the British air attacks struck terror into the people, and how they dug themselves in, hardening their hearts and losing their sense of humor in brutish survival. He had no wish to back Smith's claims, for fear of being asked whether his daughter and son-in-law might have more information. Since their last meeting he had not stopped agonizing over the news of the German invasion. Nobody in the west doubted that it would happen sooner or later, but until now nothing had transpired.

"When do you think they'll attack the Soviet Union, Howard?" Kelly did not beat around the bush.

"It was supposed to have taken place back in May, but they're still dithering, it seems, or perhaps they'll call the whole thing off, as they did with their plans to invade your island. Stalin refuses to discuss the subject, apparently. The man is completely paranoid, according to our embassy in Moscow. He doesn't trust anyone or anything, he's fixated on his pact with Hitler. We warned him some time ago, but aside from the fact that he doesn't trust us Americans, he seems to think that you English are out to draw him into the war. And you must admit, two war fronts would be to your advantage."

Kelly gave a cautious nod. "They say the Germans are massing those troops in the east to put pressure on the Russians so they'll stick to their side of the bargain. After all, Howard, half the German economy hinges on Russian resources. You know as well as I do how badly they need their grain and oil. The supplies crossing the border every day are gigantic."

"That's German propaganda for you, David. Don't you believe it, because the real reason is that they intend to go in and get that oil and grain from where it comes from. If the Russians were to mobilize now, Hitler might yet back off. Or in any case there would be a delay, because until now his trump card has been the surprise attack: he conquered half of Europe as it slept. Which is why it is crucial to know exactly when the Germans are going to invade. But Stalin has had untold numbers of his army officers murdered, and nearly all his generals are either dead or in prison. That man has brought his own army to its knees! They may not even be capable of mobilizing, I fear."

Oscar listened in silence. He had to summon all his willpower not to intervene: David, Howard, listen to me, I know, I know the date, I have the most reliable information of all, the date is set, June 22, Howard, David, Björn, June 22. Three weeks from now.

Who could he take into his confidence, here in Berne? Who would believe him, and why would they? Warn the Russians, but how? He had never met any of their embassy staff, who kept very much to themselves. Telling anyone at all was impossible, it would instantly point the finger at Emma and Carl. Their meeting in Geneva had, without a doubt, been filed in a report. The conversation between him and Emma had not been overheard by the man with the cigarette, of that he was confident, but the fact remained that they had lowered their voices. One more blot on their record. Prinz-Albrecht-Strasse disapproved of whispering.

Smith leaned back expansively in his chair.

"There are more than one hundred and fifty divisions ready and waiting, as I gathered from the Italian military attaché. There is talk of three and a half million, an unimaginable world force. We have seen them leaving *en masse* from the train stations and pouring from the west through Berlin. I have never seen so many troops as in the past few months. And they weren't heading for England, Kelly, they were going in the opposite direction. All this has nothing to do with maneuvers in faraway places beyond the reach of the R.A.F., as suggested by Herr Goebbels at his latest press conference. The Nazis produce a permanent flow of disinformation, they're very good at that. When a Nazi breathes he lies. And the Russians pretend everything is fine, they just keep harping on about the strength of their pact with the German government. There have been hints about new negotiations. Nonsense. It will happen this month, you mark my words."

Oscar listened with intent, painfully conscious of his own duplicity. He glanced around the table, saw how they were all ears for Smith. He became aware of the rumble of traffic on the Schifflaube, a comforting sound, which shifted his thoughts. Berne was the epitome of reassurance, a miracle of civilization. On a previous occasion Smith had told him how the appalling dinginess of Berlin fell away from him the moment he set foot in Switzerland. The ordinariness of Berne was a marvel to anyone coming from Germany. The shops were well stocked, there were no lines, the cafés were full, there was dining and dancing—unthinkable just a few hundred miles away. A mere train journey between them and a dark, sinister, decaying city with sirens screaming at all hours.

Oscar had been living in Berne for two years, but had yet to adapt himself to that cool city. The miles-long mall hosted a mercantile spirit that he did not share. At moments of disenchantment he remembered his boyhood history lessons, about the Swiss being soldiers for personal gain, best known for fighting other people's wars. Europe's cash register. Not a charitable thought. He knew plenty of "good" Swiss. As odd as it seemed, though, he preferred Berlin. Not the Berlin of today, the Berlin of the days when Kate and he were living there. They had left just in time, of course, the terror was escalating by the day, but to him, at that time, there had been electricity in the air, nothing was lukewarm or gray. Kate and he lived their lives in balance, without many words. Emma had left home, and Kate was working in a hospital as a theater assistant. They would arrange to meet at the bar of the Adlon after work, or at Horcher's or at Hotel Kessel. Places favored by journalists, artists and diplomats.

At the behest of his embassy, Oscar had set about establishing contact with people who were against the regime. They were easily found, for their number was directly linked to the takings of the Adlon bar. It was there that he was introduced to Adriaan Wapenaar, with whom he struck up a particular friendship, and who had reminded him quite recently that, should there be any trouble, Emma was to go to him for help. Wapenaar, a flamboyant Dutchman, had an extraordinary talent for eluding censure, even from the Gestapo. Since the outbreak of war he operated under the Swedish flag. His wife was German, and he provided assistance to the Dutch in Berlin, of whom there were thousands. Although Emma was a German citizen by law, Oscar was relieved to know Wapenaar could be relied on in an emergency.

Shortly before their return to Holland, Oscar went in search of Wapenaar at the Adlon, where he more or less held court.

"How do you rate Carl Regendorf, Adriaan?"

"A hundred percent reliable, a good German, the best of his year at the Foreign Office. Not a party member, and yet, miraculously, taken on. Why do you ask?"

"My daughter is in love with him, and he with her, and things are moving rapidly. Regendorf spends all his free time at Fasanenstrasse. Kate isn't too sure about this. Having a German in the house these days is not exactly the most desirable of farewell gifts. I can see it all go wrong, I mean, I think Emma and he are going to get married."

At that moment he realized that Wapenaar's wife was German.

"O.K., Adriaan, I know what I must sound like, but your marriage predates 1933, so that doesn't count."

Wapenaar roared with laughter. People at nearby tables smiled: cheery Hollanders, infectious fun.

Then he became serious.

"You're quite right, Oscar. It's becoming insupportable here. You're lucky, you can leave. I can't, nor do I want to, really, because of Elka and her family. We must keep in touch, you and I. We don't know when we might need each other. Where will your next posting be?"

"Nowhere for now. We'll be spending a year or so in The Hague, drifting on the tides of bureaucracy."

Wapenaar nodded. He raised his glass.

The clink of glasses jogged Verschuur's attention. He was prone to drifting into daydreams at the most poignant moments. Lifting his glass automatically, he tapped it to that of his neighbor. *Skål*, Björn. To your good health, David. *Zum Wohl*, Horst. The echo of sincere fellowship, the heartfelt cheers of like-minded friends. Smith, Henderson, Kelly and the others, united in their loathing of the forces bearing down on them: the Thousand-Year Reich.

Warn the Russians? Oscar repeated the question to himself. How trustworthy were they? Wouldn't they make inquiries about him among their German embassy friends, and, while they were at it, mention that it was he who had tipped them off about a so-called invasion? Or they might take him for some Dutch boy-scout type. A man with an obscure doctorate in history, whose career was a virtual blank and whose function and mission remained unclear. Get Smith to deliver a letter to Wapenaar, who could then leak the information via Sweden? No, that would mean shifting the onus to Smith while it was his to bear, and besides, Smith would be searched at the border. What about Björn Henderson, couldn't he share Emma's news with him? He hesitated. Much as he liked and trusted Henderson, the Swedes were cautious in the extreme. His information would doubtless be dismissed as unconfirmed rumor by the wary ambassador.

No, he would not burden Henderson.

Sending word to his ministry in London was a nonstarter. It was the last thing he would do. London was synonymous with bungling, infighting, red tape. The Dutch government-in-exile, established there in 1940, was in his opinion singularly inept. Organizing anything whatsoever via that channel was simply unacceptable. The disheartening exchanges with them in the line of duty were bad enough. What he was doing in Switzerland was of his own devising and initiative: activities off the beaten track, operations that would have scandalized the penpushers at Stratton House or in Ascot or wherever their desks were nowadays. Had they known, they would have been running to their bosses, clamoring for him to be stopped.

Oscar Martinus Verschuur, Ph.D., having earned his doctorate with a thesis on a pack of Zulu warriors, was an important link in Switzerland for refugees trying to get into the country. Most of the people he helped were French or German, and now and again a few Dutch. And London was not involved in any of that. They had no idea. Wapenaar in Berlin knew, so did the Dutch consul in Lugano. And Kate. But of the hundred or so people of assorted nationalities whom he had managed to smuggle over the border, not a single one knew him, or at least not his name, nor those of his few contacts in Holland and Belgium. He had become the Dutch Foreign Ministry's consummate cover-up agent. Which was why nobody ever made the connection between him and Morton. Morton was in the know, he was kept informed of developments by Oscar, who acted mainly on Morton's instructions. Major Desmond Morton, intelligence adviser to Winston Churchill. "Mystery Morton," as Smith referred to him, but to Oscar there was nothing mysterious about the man whose acquaintance he and Wapenaar had made in Berlin, early in '38.

Morton had done his homework. He knew exactly who they were, their backgrounds, their reputation for hard-headedness. He mentioned the names of people both Oscar and Wapenaar trusted. He wanted to know whether they would be willing to work with him in the future. Morton was deeply pessimistic as to what that future held. What they saw happening in Germany was the beginning of a catastrophe on a global scale—oh no, he was not exaggerating. That was why he was assembling a shadow-army all over Europe, men and women Britain could mobilize if the need arose. A mammoth game of chess. They had declared themselves willing. That they would both have risen so high in the ranks by the time the need arose was something Morton had not foreseen, but for the rest his forecasts had come true with chilling accuracy. He had presented them with the scenario as of a family feud, listing one by one the countries that would be occupied by Germany. Only in the case of Sweden, which Germany had left alone, had he got it wrong. Switzerland's neutrality was just as he had predicted, and quite evident, given the close ties between the Nazis and Europe's treasure chest. All the better. Both Verschuur and Wapenaar were able to provide him with valuable intelligence. For his sake they were prepared to risk offending their respective ministries. Morton, Churchill's confidant, was at one with them. Blind faith was the watchword, untarnished until the present.

Morton was his best chance, the only person he could dare to discuss the impending operation with. He should have realized from the first, but now his mind was made up. He could trust the Englishman to ensure that the information would never be traced to him and his daughter. He felt a surge of relief: free at last to join in the conversation.

"Have you heard the news about Bishop von Galen?" Smith said. Oscar had seen the name in the papers. *Die Nation* had recently devoted a long article to the remarkable churchman, who had shown the temerity to voice his protest in public. Protest, a word the Germans couldn't even spell anymore.

"All the crucifixes had to be removed from Bavarian classrooms. Orders of one Doctor Meyer, some local bigwig in lederhosen, I presume. Mind you, that von Galen protested to Hitler! Never happened before, someone complaining to Wotan in person. And that was not all, there were people demonstrating in the street, and rumor has it that Hitler was jeered at in Bavaria, although that is something I find hard to believe."

Henderson broke in: "We heard that story too. But they can carry on hanging crucifixes in the schools, because the order was rescinded. It was a mistake, Goebbels said. Not a good moment to rile the Catholics, probably. So long as they can carry on hanging Jews—now there's something they should be protesting against, instead of making a fuss about wooden crosses in the classroom!"

Henderson was not Roman Catholic, presumably. Jewish perhaps? Indignant in any case. His anger and sarcasm struck a chord with Oscar, recalling the rage that possessed himself at times, the powerlessness, the anguish over Emma in Berlin. This amicable gathering of diplomats was merely a brief interlude of distraction.

They plied Smith with questions, whose replies were duly commented upon and expanded. He was a messenger from the Underworld, on short leave, witness to events which were taking place just outside the others' grasp and yet almost close enough to touch. An exasperating state of affairs to the diplomatic frame of mind, although they abided by Goethe's rule: judge by what you see, and respect the unseen. Goethe, the giant whose lifework lay unread, the intellectual locomotive of the old Germany with all those quarrelsome kings and counts and dukes and generals and bishops. That it should come to this, in the land of Goethe . . . a refrain of lament over the land that once brought forth heroes of such greatness, not that anybody knew what that greatness stood for. People simply parroted one another, perpetuating the myths. The land of Goethe, what of it? The land of Alfred Rosenberg and Goering more like it, the land of stupidity and death. A play in three acts: the rise, the flowering, and the downfall of the Idiot.

Oscar respected the unseen, certainly. It was his lifeblood. But not now.

It was well past midnight by the time he trudged up the Schifflaube on his way home.

Chapter 6

Kate woke up early, as usual: a habit left over from when Emma was a toddler. She had lost the ability to sleep late. London was hushed and still, the light of morning barely perceptible. Wednesday, June 4: Emma's birthday. The first quarter-hour of the day, when she surfaced from dreams that more often than not were disturbing. She was a dreamer, making up at night for what she missed during the day. Passion and common sense were opposite sides of the same coin in her case, some would say. She herself did not go in for such introspection. Fifteen minutes to recover from sleep, her arms and legs feeling heavy, her musings and sentiments as light as air. Emma, Carl, Oscar. Matteous. The silkiness of the name as pronounced by him, the African tone and lilt of it, were impossible to emulate, but the echo of it rang in her ears. She had left him behind in his lodgings the day before, restraining herself from taking him home with her. The rain pelting down on Earls Court Road had not made for a cheerful scene. The way each of them had kept silent in that small room overlooking the busy street said enough: what am I doing here, is this where you want me to be, I can't stay forever, nobody knows me, I no longer exist.

Thinking back, Kate recalled Matteous's ice-cold hands, and his disconsolate look when she broke the silence at last with some favorable comment on his room.

Fifteen minutes in bed in the quiet of earliest morning, a delicate mechanism affording her a leisurely adjustment to the passing of time. One hand on her stomach, the other under her head: an attitude of surrender to an unknown love, of a lover at a loss. She had no commitments, nothing more to prove, it all lay behind her, youth, marriage, motherhood. All there was now was the war, and a black boy who had unaccountably come into her life. Should she go and see him later on, or should she leave him alone? Matteous was no longer a child, and she not his mother, though it seemed a lot like it at times. Emma had grown up so fast that Kate had hardly had a chance to be a mother. Now, at fifty-four, she wondered what on earth she had spent all that time doing. For some reason everything had seemed to happen at high speed. Like watching the water drain out of a basin when you pulled the plug. The little whirlpool at the plughole, that was where she was now.

Somewhere in the neighborhood a clock struck six. In Berlin the day would also be beginning. Their clocks were an hour ahead, of course, so Carl would be on the train by now. Matteous would still be asleep, she imagined. And so would Oscar, almost certainly. She did not think about Oscar very much lately. She registered this as a curious state of affairs, not as a cause for concern. They lived their lives much as sparrows perching on the same clothes line: fairly content, fairly tame. Their embrace seemed to have lost its necessity, and the distance between Berne and London did not make them yearn for one another. This suited Kate quite well, it was just fine. Eros had never played a big part in their lives, which was probably true of a lot of people. The years before Oscar did not count,

for they lay dormant in her core. Or as good as dormant. Sometimes, rarely, very rarely, they came back to her in a dream or in
her fifteen-minute reverie upon waking.

There had been a change over the past months, since she
had met Matteous. It happened several times that she was jolted
awake by the crash, her heart thumping. The terrifying crash.
After the fear came the memory, and with the memory the
pain. She was eighteen again and just married. She was back
in Rome, holding hands with him as they wandered through
the old city. He was working on the Roman Forum excavations, his "never-ending dustpan-and-brush project," as he
called it. One of the most talented archaeologists of his genera-
tion, older than her by ten years: Roy de Winther, Winther with
an *h*. Countless times she had spelled it out—Winther with an *h*
after the *t*—during their years of European travel. Four years to
be precise. From Gibraltar to Oslo, from Budapest and Kiev
to Rome and Sicily. There were always archaeological finds to
be inspected, museums that were not to be missed, conferences
and special seminars to be attended. Sometimes they rented a
house where Roy could work on his lectures and write articles
for international journals and newspapers. Once Schliemann
had discovered Troy, archaeological excavations became news-
worthy, and archaeologists were much in demand. Roy de
Winther was among those in demand. Also from Kate, especially from her. Her willfulness had taken him by storm, and
within half a year they were married. The past was his concern,
the future would be hers. Their immediate future consisted of
traveling. Having a child did not enter her mind, she felt little
more than a child herself. All those trains, cars, ships, all those
hotels and pensions, rented accommodations, cultural insti-
tutes . . . It was the carefree time before the Great War, a period
of vigor and ambition. They were part of it all, their energy was

boundless, they were free spirits, they were crazy about each other. The world would never be the same again, no love, no death would ever be the same. No measure of devotion or happiness could compare with the experience they shared during those years.

Kate had covered it all up, stowed everything away in sealed packages wrapped around by the new life she found herself leading after the catastrophe. Four years of undivided devotion should be enough to keep the machines of memory in fuel forever. But the machines had let her down, the memories of those days began to fade, or were quickly pushed out of sight. She had proved able to make his body vanish, and forget his love. Concrete it over.

But nothing vanishes for good. Not the train journey, which was Roy's last. From Milan to Rome and her. The crash had to have been horrific, the newspapers carried pictures of great mounds of twisted steel, of flames and chaos and passengers trapped in the wreckage. Sixty dead. Roy was mentioned by name in the reports. She still had the newspaper somewhere. Stored away, like all the rest.

Time to get up: she was due at the hospital, the boys would be waiting for her, including Matteous, perhaps. She had to move her arms and legs, get away from the old, dead, illusory world of her dreams. Roy's world, her husband's.

June 4: Emma's twenty-ninth birthday. Kate wondered briefly if her daughter would be celebrating it, and if so how. She opened the blackout curtains. The sun was rising, and soon the rumble of traffic would be heard on Earls Court Road, where the buses went past Matteous's lodgings. Birds began to sing, a gardener began to rake the gravel in the square nearby. Without much thought, Kate reckoned with the possibility of an air raid, although it had been quiet for a fortnight now.

She kept a bucket filled with water in the kitchen. Symbolic instance of preparedness: a midge's tiny fist raised against a leviathan.

When she rang at his studio there was no answer. No footfalls, no throat-clearing, not even a whisper. Not a sound. She rang again, longer and more insistently. Again silence; the door remained closed. She took a few steps back to the edge of the pavement and looked up. He was standing in the shadows, as far away from the window as possible, almost like a statue, with a streak of sunlight falling across his dark head. That was how she had seen him when she came to pick him up from the hospital ward. He appeared not to notice her, he was not at home, the bell had not rung, the unmistakable, alarming shrill had gone unheard. Kate wanted to call out to him and wave, but then thought better of it. She regretted having disturbed him by coming to his door. He was practicing not being there, adopting the stance of a soldier who has been killed, but doesn't know it yet. The final seconds before falling, the bullets lodged already in the body. Nonsense of course, she was just imagining things, going over the top, like a bad film. What she was seeing was impossible. He just stood there. Standing had become second nature to him. Standing ready, standing on guard, standing in the never-ending drill of the platoon, forever in formation. That was all it was, she was not to jump to any conclusions. She would not disturb him.

Kate began to walk away, in the direction of the bus stop for Richmond Royal Hospital, when a shout from above reached her ears.

"Miss!"

The urgency was unmistakable. She stopped, spun around and waved at Matteous, who was leaning out of the window, beckoning her.

Inside, the wicker suitcase was still in exactly the same place. Nothing in the room had changed since she had left him there the day before. As if that day had not passed into night and then day again, as if he had not moved from where he stood. No need for blackout if you don't switch the light on. All safe, all right and proper, the room in complete darkness and invisible to the enemy. Kate asked no questions. She sat down on the only chair. Matteous remained standing. His eyes were darker than ever, the whites almost gray. Inclining his head, he struggled to frame a sentence. And another. His English sounded as if he were groping his way across a rope bridge. His hands supported his words, his shoulders leaned from side to side. Did Miss think he would be going home to the Congo? They had obviously forgotten about him in the army, and the Belgian government-in-exile couldn't care less about an injured Congolese stranded in London. He wanted to find his mother. His mother. The big word his life had orbited around for months, for years. His mother, who had been captured and who might not be dead. The mother he had been forced to leave behind when his father told him to run for his life. Quick as a flash he had run, as fast as an antelope.

Kate put her hand on his sleeve, saying, "Of course," although she had no idea if such a thing was possible. A soldier being discharged from hospital to free up much-needed space—would that mean he was discharged from the army, too? Probably not, but she didn't even want to consider the question. Matteous's enemy was completely different from everybody else's. He had fought without any idea of who he was fighting against. Caught up in a war of strangers against strangers, in a conflict whose causes and aims were beyond his grasp. He had drifted into the army because he had lost his family, because he had to go somewhere, anywhere, to avoid dying of heartache.

And he had rescued that officer to avoid having to flee into the jungle all over again. Strong enough at last to hoist a man on his shoulders, away from the frontline and the bloodshed, without fear. In the jumble of French, English and Swahili, Kate could hear his grief about his mother. She took his hand, enclosed it in both of hers, and lifted the three hands to her chest for a moment, the way he always did in greeting. The dark hand, the dark face so close to hers.

Chapter 7

Carl sang her a sweet birthday ditty in German and gave her a hug, then pulled back the curtains and opened the window. The birds would do the rest of the singing, he said. The weather was warm, perfect for a birthday celebration. Friends would be arriving later that evening, as many as twenty. They would all be bringing some food. Drink, too.

Carl left for work later than usual. The previous evening they had stayed up late, going over and over what the Gestapo might and might not know. Emma was sick with worry about her father, while Carl was becoming increasingly nervous on her account. He tried not to show it, but he was besieged by a constant, light form of panic. They had a file on her, they were watching her. Which meant that he too was being watched, as well as Trott. They had fallen asleep holding hands, worn out from all their speculations.

Emma saw him to the garden gate, and watched as he walked down the road, their rural byroad on the outskirts of the violence. His train would take him to the unimaginable amphitheater of crime: a free performance, all day long. She would not focus on that, it was too overwhelming. The events were

beyond her. She inhaled the fragrance of the June gardens all
around, and tried to follow Carl in her mind once he was out of
sight, boarding the train, leaving Dahlem toward the city center. She wanted to hang on to his physical presence, the body
in which she had nestled herself. But that was a dream, wish-
ful thinking. There he was, walking away from her, without
her, thinking ahead to what might await him at his office. He
might spare a thought for her now and then, recalling how she
had returned his embrace. And had sighed about getting old:
"Twenty-nine, Carl, I'm twenty-nine now, don't you think I'm
old?" He had said it was the world that was old, not her.

She had a busy day ahead: tidy up the house, unpack those
bags that had been blocking the hall for the past two days, go to
the few shops that still had anything left to sell, lay the table for
twenty people. As if nothing was the matter, as if it was the most
normal thing in the world to celebrate one's birthday. Come
what may. Well, twenty people were coming. Their friends
from Dahlem, a few from Zehlendorf, a few from the city center, and even somebody from Potsdam, who would be staying
the night—they might all end up staying the night, if there was
an air-raid warning. She had seen the devastation from the car
window on the way to Prinz-Albrecht-Strasse. Entire streets
lay in ruins. After a while she had lost her bearings, in spite of
being quite familiar with the city. She had lived there as a stu-
dent for almost four years, from August 1931 till June 12, 1933,
the day of her finals, after which she had left immediately. A
few weeks before that she had been in the Opernplatz together
with some friends, watching transfixed as books were being
burned. The S.A. men were in a frenzy, leaping and shouting
as they set upon the piles of books and hurled them onto the
bonfire. It had felt like a rehearsal for mass murder. Where they
burn books, they will end in burning human beings: the lesson

of Heinrich Heine, whose work had gone up in smoke with all the rest that evening. Her studies at the university had not posed any problems. "If you want to study history in the making, go to Berlin," she had been told in Holland. A sound piece of advice. The windows of the lecture halls on Unter den Linden rattled to the noise of demonstrations and parades and police charges and countercharges going on outside. She needed only to glance out of the window to see history unfold. If the professors were to be believed, you could hear the groundwork being laid for a thousand-year empire.

The ride in the car, she had relived it dozens of times. Not a long ride, half an hour at the most, but enough for night after night without sleep. The two Gestapo men, no more than boys really, had sat one in the front and one in the back with her. They paid no attention to her, asked no questions. They looked as if they had just stepped out of a shop selling Gestapo uniforms: shiny coats, shiny shoes, shiny pistols. But the car was old and battered, and reeked of stale cigarette smoke. The driver clearly enjoyed taking corners at speed. Emma kept having to reach out for support, and several times her hand had brushed against the arm of the boy beside her. The roads of Dahlem were excellent for tearing around corners. Falkenried, then left, In der Halde, turn right, Am Hirschsprung, right again up the Dohnenstieg. Had they taken the Dohnenstieg for a particular reason? Did they know Himmler lived there? A bit of racing past the boss's house? They knew the way by heart; one more short cut and they came to the Lenzeallee. Full speed ahead to their robbers' den.

Emma felt treated like a criminal, though she acted as if she were being driven to an appointment. These boys were not going to detect the slightest nervousness on her part. She peered out of the window with interest, twisted around for a backward glance, turned her head from side to side, opened her handbag with a casual air. The relaxed gestures of a day out sightseeing. It was imperative that she keep her rising panic under control. How extraordinary that the city was functioning again after the heavy bombardments, as if they had never happened. Traffic was as hectic as ever, with buses, trams, carts, motor cars, pavements milling with people. She saw a clock on the Potsdamer Platz, which was quite near where she used to live. It was still intact, hands pointing to a quarter past eleven. A telling detail. The clocks were right, it was business as usual, trains and trams on time, arrests made on schedule. Gestapo at the ready, motor running. It was clear the orders were for her to be picked up at eleven and brought in at half past.

"Emma Regendorf-Verschuur, where were you yesterday?"

The somber man questioning her tried his best to be civil. A form of civility that could turn nasty in an instant. He resembled a boxer in a jacket, sleeves bulging with muscles, ready to let fly at any moment.

"In Geneva, with my husband and his head of department, Herr Adam von Trott of the Foreign Office. But why do you ask? And why am I here? I should like to call my husband."

The man facing her said nothing. This could hardly be called an interrogation, it had more of a sequence of silences with the occasional query thrown in, a smirk, a sigh, a cigarette being lit, a weary gesture. And the constant tapping of a shoe on the floor.

Emma looked past the man into a tiny courtyard, or rather a shaft, which admitted some daylight. Such a sad little nook, overlooked by the architect, a hole with no purpose other than to deepen the gloom of the surroundings. The silence and murkiness of the building began to oppress her. She felt the fear welling up again. Everyone in Germany knew about this address, this place where she now was. Everyone avoided this street. The pavements were deserted, the entire premises radiated menace. How in heaven's name could she make her escape, what kind of attitude should she take? She forced herself to think of her father, which calmed her down somewhat. All this was about him—she had realized that at the first question. Not about Carl or Adam, thank goodness. Not yet. Her father was safe in Switzerland, for the time being anyway. She had not thought of him as someone important enough to be watched by the Gestapo. Her father, whom she looked up to and dearly loved but never felt she really understood. The unusual relationship between her parents perplexed her periodically, but it remained a mystery. Harmonious for the most part, openminded, alert, witty, but on the edges there was loneliness. They both seemed to have distanced themselves, or else outgrown each other.

"What is your father's occupation in Switzerland?" the lugubrious man said, his tone making it clear that he did not expect her to tell the truth.

She replied curtly that he worked at the Dutch embassy in Berne and that she didn't know exactly what his job entailed. "My father didn't discuss his work much at home."

The man leered at her. He probably didn't discuss his work much at home either, Emma thought in a flash of grim amusement. The fear receded. She had to get away from there, and quickly.

They had made her wait for two hours in a sort of kitchen-cum-cloakroom, without anybody looking at her twice. People went in and out, fetched coffee, hung their coats up and generally ignored her. And there, in that poky space, she had been overwhelmed by thoughts of Watse, her dearest friend in Holland. Watse Hepkema, the boy she grew up with, the boy executed a few months ago by these people's partners in crime. Watse, shot without trial for resisting. There, between those walls, she felt his death as if it were taking place in the next room. The news had left her stunned for days, unable to take it in. He had urged her so many times to get out of "that rotten city, that rotten country," as soon as possible, and to tell Carl he had no business being there either. Watse had been her closest tie with Holland, and now he was dead. The images came back to her. Watse, arrested and shot, allegedly while trying to escape, not long after the Tour of 1941, which he had done on ice-hockey skates because his speed skates had been stolen—the blades on which no one could touch him. When the wind was against them he would skate in front of her, he was as strong as a bear. Her memory of their last expeditions over the Sneekermeer was as fresh as yesterday, and his question continued to gnaw at the back of her mind: "Is Carl still working for those gangsters?" Yes, he was. Slowly, far too slowly, she had begun to realize that they were trapped. It was impossible for Carl to leave. There was no way he could emigrate, let alone switch sides. Every person on German soil was lost. Marriage to a German meant that she was German too, someone regarded with suspicion, someone who had to line up endlessly with a coupon for this and a coupon for that. Emma's love of Carl was undiminished, but her sense of isolation weighed more heavily by the day. Friends from Holland stopped writing, relatives fell silent, only within Carl's circle was there any respite. Germans, pigs? Not Trott, not Langbehn, not Haeften, but so many others: yes. Was it true about the German Foreign Office being a breeding ground of resistance, as Carl and Trott maintained? She found it hard to believe. Watse's opinion was probably closer to the truth. He was a Frisian, and a skater beyond compare. She treasured her memory of skating with him over the frozen lakes of Sneek and

Gaastmeer back in the winter of 1938, when they were practicing for the Eleven Cities Tour. Not a soul ahead of them, clear ice as hard as marble. She had made the trip especially from Berlin. Carl had sputtered a little, but she had appealed to their bond of childhood friendship. The kind of bond that whenever little Emma was asked who her friends were, Watse's was always the first name to come up. It was late in December that she received a telegram from him saying "ELEVEN CITIES TOUR, YOUR PRESENCE URGENTLY REQUIRED." She couldn't let Watse skate the whole course on his own, it wouldn't be fair.

And so she went, three months after the phony Munich Agreement, which professed peace, but which stank of war. It was a wrench leaving Carl behind, but Emma was delighted to escape the menaced and menacing city for a while.

They skated side by side through the polders toward the frozen Sneekermeer, Watse on speed skates, Emma wearing the traditional strap-on type, on which she was as graceful as she was swift. The low sun in their eyes, frosted reeds in tufts on the banks, a bridge here, a hole hacked in the ice for ducks there, they danced their way to Sneek. Same rhythm, same strokes, same style, although Watse slowed down a fraction. The first goal was reached without any pause or hesitation: the Pavilion on the edge of the Sneekermeer. They had gone to sit by the window overlooking the lake, with skating figures in the distance silhouetted against a cloudless sky: a frozen landscape resembling a painting by Avercamp or the meticulous Schelfhout, masters of the Dutch winter scene. Watse had looked at her searchingly, it was such a long time since they had spoken.

"How are things over there, Emma, are you coping all right? Is Carl still working for those gangsters?"

Subtlety was not his trademark. Honesty was. A man of few words, but when he did say something it was usually worth hearing.

His question sounded like a pistol shot. Emma knew he liked Carl well enough; he had come to visit them once in Dahlem, and they had agreed on many issues. Carl had told him about the efforts he and Trott were making to get in touch with whoever was against the Nazis. Watse had left, taciturn as ever, and downcast.

"Do you remember us playing in the park, when a boy got hold of me and threw me over? You were there in a trice. You grabbed him and pushed him in the pond. And fished him out again. I believe I considered that quite normal at the time, but from then on I knew I had nothing to fear as long as I was with you. If worst comes to worst, Carl and I will come hide at your place, all right?" Emma laughed, putting her hand on his arm. "So stay right where you are, Watse, and don't look so serious."

In retrospect, their skating trip on the frozen Sneekermeer had been one of the most glowing, light-hearted days of her life. They had skated as never before, nimbly and fast, Watse and she close together, hands clasped behind their backs, the sun just above the reeds, the sky like a dome over the countryside. The world was cast in ice, and it was theirs, theirs alone. Legs, feet, and wide, gliding strokes, nothing more. There was hardly any wind, the ice was hard and dry, no cracks or ridges. Late in the afternoon, when the sun had almost gone and darkness began to fall over the landscape, they stopped. Carrying their skates in their hands, they set off toward a bus stop. Half past four, and they could hear the bus approaching from a mile's distance. Fields stretched away in dark, chessboard squares as the brightly lit vehicle floated toward them. Watse waved; they got on. But it felt as if they were on the bus in body only, not in mind, for they were children again playing on the embankment until Mrs. Hepkema called for them to come indoors.

At long last, the lugubrious man led her via a double-doored lock-chamber into a slightly larger space, as sparsely furnished as the changing room of a public swimming pool. A few uniforms hung from the pegs on the walls, in the middle stood a gray metal desk with a wooden chair on either side. It was deathly quiet; the double doors were soundproof.

Once the dumb play and trivial opening questions were over, Emma felt her throat tighten, as if all the air were being sucked out of the room. She had to get out of there, do something. She stood up, looked the boxer in the eye and said: "I have nothing more to say. I should like to go now, if you don't mind, or else please make a telephone call to Herr von Trott at the foreign office."

Her tone was clear, almost casual, self-possessed.

The shoe-tapping ceased, the cigarette was stubbed out in the metal ashtray, the jacket given a tug, the chair pushed back.

"Your mother . . ."

Of the few sentences uttered by the ghoul this was the one that kept coming back to her. A dirty-minded little man being provocative. Or was there more to it? It had sounded almost accusing, about her mother being quite a looker. In the Gestapo's eyes, of course, the same eyes that had been ogling her breasts during their cozy exchange.

When she finally stood outside again, her bag slung over her shoulder, she noticed how chilled she felt in the warm air. The June light and the summer heat had been abruptly cut off upon entering the building. A few hours of isolation and bewilderment and exposure to insulting manners were enough to turn her world upside down. She set off along Prinz-Albrecht-Strasse, then broke into a run, only to slow down after a few paces because it would attract too much attention: nobody ran like that. She paused to catch her breath, leaning against the wall of a shop with tears running down her face as she wept over Watse, over Carl, over everything. A man passing by eyed her with concern and asked if she needed help, but she waved him off. The show of kindness was exceptional: people tended to shun one another in the street, at least until the next bombing raid, when they would rally together and help each other to their feet.

Carl would be on his train by now, Emma reflected. She was still leaning against the garden gate, absorbed in what she now thought of as her kidnapping. Kidnapped in broad daylight by a couple of upstarts, and subjected to questioning by a loathsome thug. She had made out to Carl that she had slept well. She had not told him how undone she was over the arrest and interrogation, how worried about her father, how Watse's death had hit her all over again. She did not wish to burden him unnecessarily. She had to think ahead to that evening. Would she manage to get hold of wine for her birthday dinner? And what on earth should she cook, she didn't have near enough ration cards. Slowly, Emma bestirred herself. Household concerns took over, such as shopping—especially shopping. She wondered how her mother would have dealt with providing a meal for twenty guests. Her mother was experienced in such matters, her parents were always having people to dinner: mixed parties of diplomats, journalists, with some figures from the art world thrown in. She had never seen her mother truly enjoying herself in the role of hostess; even as a child she had felt that it was her father who was behind all the entertaining. Her mother did her part, but with a certain reserve. Her mother, who was considered quite a looker by the Gestapi, as Carl always referred to them. That her father was involved in clandestine dealings was not surprising, though it had never occurred to her that the Nazis were having him followed everywhere. But her mother, what could she have to do with anything? Her mother lived in London, and surely the Germans weren't cracked enough to have a spy reporting on her appearance. So it had to be a report from a while back, the time they had gone skiing together. But that was more than a year ago. Were they already watching him then? Everything worried her, her thoughts flying in all directions. And she didn't even want to think, all she wanted was to go and do her shopping, stand in some endless line, say hello to the next-door neighbor, sweep the doorstep if need be.

"Dear friends." Carl stood up, glass in hand. It took a while for the chatter to die down at the long table linking the front and back rooms. The twenty guests sitting shoulder to shoulder gave an impression of resoluteness. They rallied themselves.

"Dear friends, welcome to this house of abundance. You have all contributed marvelously. I counted a dozen omelets, five sandwiches, twenty plates of soup, seven heads of lettuce, one cucumber, two loaves of bread, and twenty napkins—take care, the latter are not edible."

Carl spoke as if it were peacetime. The late sun made the wine sparkle in the glasses raised to Emma.

"My dearest Emma, here is to you, to another year with you. May the war be over by the end of it, may we all be gathered together again a year from now."

Glasses were clinked, smiles were beamed at Emma and Carl, it was like a wedding feast. In the middle of war, in the middle of Germany, could it be true that they were all there while pretending to be elsewhere? Emma felt for Carl's hand

and squeezed it under the table. Their lives had gone underground, their love was not intended for the eyes of others. Everything beyond this room and this company of friends had become suspect.

Opposite Emma sat Adam Trott. All the guests knew each other well, there was not a shred of mistrust, a safer ambience was hard to imagine. He rose to his feet. Adam, the tireless mediator between the most miscellaneous opponents of the regime. A troupe of individuals scattered by the storm, keeping their heads down until further notice, biding their time with dreams of freedom.

Adam was an optimist. Emma admired him for what Carl had told her about him, but more for him as a person. She heard him evoke the Germany of his youth, for which he was so intensely nostalgic. That Germany had been stolen from them, but it still existed, smoldering underground as a moorland fire. With a lover's zeal, he entreated his audience not to forsake their country.

She had not known him to make such an impassioned speech before. He was not addressing her in particular, although he had begun by putting his arm around her and offering his congratulations. A hush had fallen. Adam did not raise his voice, but each word was charged with electricity. He conjured an ideal vision which was common to them all, because they had forged it together; he lifted the curtain on their workaday hardship, revealing the pitiful circumstances in which they were forced to live: the lack of justice in the law courts, the overweening callousness, the snitching that had become the norm, the dearth of all hope and love. Sweeping statements, to be sure, but despite the pathos and the rhetoric, Adam spoke with such conviction that they had to believe him. Shoulder to shoulder, glasses aloft, that fourth day of June, 1941, had felt like a triumph of sorts, a foretaste of what was to come, what would ultimately be theirs.

The evening was perfect, the best Emma had ever had in Germany. Adam was applauded, his eyes shone, he had the air of a soldier called up for service and eager for battle. And with reason: he felt himself a soldier, for all that his battles were fought without guns. The ministries in Berlin were caught up in a guerrilla war between administrators and clerks, divisions and subdivisions, spies and counter-spies. Adam found his arm being twisted by Himmler's minions on a daily basis.

But on the evening of Emma's birthday, with the sun's heat lingering in the gardens of Dahlem and not a single aircraft to be heard, all was clear and transparent. She felt reconciled with the way her life was going, with the empty days without Carl, the anguish of the war, the yearning for a normal existence, for children, for her father and mother. Carl was not aware of her moods of despair. She had never told him, nor had she told him about Watse's warning. This was her party, her night of radiance, free of all grudge and fear. The radio was switched on and they danced; there was a gramophone, and records of banned singers. Were the windows closed tight, and the curtains? Dancing on a volcano, feet tripping lightly over a floor of flames. *Ich bin von Kopf bis Fuss.* Until the first rays of sunshine in the morning.

Chapter 8

Apart from Lara nobody knew he was going to London. He informed his office that he was spending a few days in the mountains. Swissair B 320 took about three hours to fly to Lisbon. Once there, he had to find some way of boarding a plane to England: quite a challenge, as there was only one flight a day and many prominent individuals seeking passage. Fortunately, the name Desmond Morton worked wonders. At Lisbon Airport he was promptly assigned to an extra flight scheduled for the following evening.

Time was racing by, and Oscar's desperation grew. It had taken a whole week to get in touch with Morton, precious days in which his information was going to waste. Just as well there had been only one day's delay in Lisbon. Lisbon, a strange, forgotten city, and at the same time an international laboratory for espionage, and a small paradise for diplomats. Everyone was watching everybody else, in almost unbroken sunshine, in the Cidade da Luz, the City of Light. Should he pay a visit to his friend van Oldenborgh, who organized support for refugees? Another time perhaps, better not attract attention. He avoided the Dutch embassy for the same reason. The last time he called there he had been infuriated by the then envoy, the impossible, pedantic Sillem, the man who failed to lift a finger to help the motley crowd of stranded compatriots, simply abandoning them to their fate. Oscar couldn't abide him, neither could van Oldenborgh.

Oscar took the tram uphill to Alfama, the old fishermen's quarter in the middle of the city. From there he looked out over the River Tagus and listened to the sing-song tones of Portuguese spoken around him. A scattering of palm trees put him in mind of Africa; there was a Moorish feel to the place. But he paid little attention to his surroundings, all he wanted was to find some peaceful spot to escape the oppressive heat of the downtown area. The outdoor café he stopped at was almost empty. The sun shone on the Tagus, with its wide mouth leading out to the ocean. Cargo boats chugged upriver, fishing craft moored at the quays, pilot boats sent up curves of spray as they raced to their clients, yachts sailed leisurely to sea. It left him cold, all of it. It was as if a huge screen had been unrolled upon which the scene on the river was projected: unreal, obscure, a magic-lantern performance that had nothing to do with the real world. He heard seagulls, church bells, children playing in the alleys, the sounds of a lost age. It felt unseemly to be sitting there, as if he were shirking his duty. Which was what he had done, of course. He had tried his utmost to push Emma's news to the back of his mind, pretend she had never told him. Only when that didn't work, and the realization hit him that he had no choice but to warn Morton, had he set about booking a flight. It had all taken days and days. Morton's arm was long, but even for him Switzerland was a difficult nut to crack. In Portugal apparently he had more influence.

For the past three months Lara had occupied him without pause. Occupied was not the right word: too matter-of-fact. She held sway over him without touching, infusing every chamber of his soul with warmth. Even that was a poor description, like some old-fashioned fairytale romance; no, it would not do. Try as he might, he was unable to put his dreamed life with Lara into words. How she looked, moved, spoke, kept silent, asked a question. He felt himself the keeper of a warehouse of gestures and words, he was a repository of feelings both processed and raw. She took him back to the days before the death of his father, to an age of innocence. She was a wondrous, distant echo of the girl who had kissed him on the mouth in a fathomless past, and breathed life into him.

His memories of their first days together were all tangled up. His confusion had not abated since that day in Café Eiger and their walk the next morning—not before ten, she had said, and he had been there at ten.

"Hello, Oscar, quite a change from yesterday, isn't it?" The sun had not yet risen above the Jungfrau, which stood out against the deep blue sky in almost lurid contrast. Waiters were shoveling the snow off the terrace into banks along the edges. There was one couple having breakfast with their overcoats on, waiting for the sun to burst upon them.

"Germans," Lara muttered. "Complete fanatics." Oscar, ever on his guard, peered at them. But they seemed harmless: the man and the woman were far too showily dressed, and besides, he had only decided to go skiing on the spur of the moment two days earlier. But should he not, for his part, have made some inquiries about Lara? He dismissed the idea at once, feeling almost ashamed.

"Shall we walk to Kleine Scheidegg?" He had made the suggestion casually, as if that was what they had already agreed to do. Going to sit with her at a table again seemed a little daunting. The previous day had been the longest café-table session of his life: an avalanche of impressions as he came under the spell of the woman he was with, who had dropped from the snowy sky like a falcon on a field mouse.

Lara van Oosten, forty-one years old, whose life, according to her, seemed to be over. No children, and a boyfriend she had once loved, but whose whereabouts now were unknown. He might be dead, in fact that was quite likely. In any case, he had vanished. The story of her life. She evoked in him a sharp ache of yearning which he had not known since boyhood, when books and poems were opening up a dizzying range of possibilities, when he met the girl who whisked him away from an existence flowing calmly along its steady course. Now, age fifty-six, he found himself well and truly at sea.

He had held her hand for the last hundred yards back to her hotel, because it was slippery underfoot, and she might fall. Her hand in his for a hundred yards. That was what it all came down to: her hand had never let go. He had left her on the terrace of Hotel Jungfrau. At the very last, he had pulled her glove off her hand and held her warm palm against his cheek. A minor embrace with major consequences. Naked, the intimacy could not have been greater.

The walk from Hotel Jungfrau to Kleine Scheidegg was not steep, a mere stroll to a mountaineer, but Lara and Oscar had made their way carefully, slowly, as if they were waiting for something to happen. They had paused often. A rumbling noise coming from the side of the mountain was the echo of a small avalanche, they saw it rolling toward them in slow motion, innocently far off, in a landscape sculpted by avalanches.

Excitedly, she pointed to a group of chamois high on the flank of the Jungfrau.

"Were those goats what you were looking at with your binoculars?"

She smiled and laid her hand on his sleeve.

"Such curiosity! No, that was not what I was looking at, because they weren't there. I was trying to spot a party of mountain climbers I had talked to in the village. One of them reminded me of Harold."

She had told him about Harold, the man she had lost, to what or to whom she was not sure. The years with him had been wonderful and exciting. And they had ended as abruptly as they had begun. Three years ago she received a letter from him saying that he would not be returning to Switzerland. They had both been working in Basel when he was suddenly called away. He was a petrochemical engineer, she had a job at the university, they lived quite near each other and they had never married. Still, he had been her anchor among all those Swiss. In his last letter he said he had joined the army, special branch, he did not go into any detail. As an Englishman he could not refuse the call of duty. He had asked her to give notice to his landlord and to sell off his furniture; the proceeds were hers to keep.

"I dream about him quite regularly, always the same dream. That he's right there all of a sudden, and I want to scream at him, but no sound comes out of my mouth."

Oscar was put in mind of Kate, who had used the same terms to describe her years with Roy, her first husband: wonderful and exciting. As she had told him little else, those years had assumed mythical proportions: the prime of Kate and Roy in the gilded early years of the twentieth century. Later, she had rebuilt her life with Oscar, a life of measure, a life of appointment diaries and dinners and much waiting. Waiting for a new posting, for Emma, for news from a world in disarray. Berlin had been the watershed. Kate had cast off convention and expectation to become a theater assistant in the Charlottenburg hospital. There, the flood of insanity came pouring in by ambulance and stretcher: stab wounds, gunshot wounds, broken bones, smashed arms and legs, bleeding heads. An unending stream of casualties, victims of the violence perpetrated by the bullies against Jews or Communists. Kate knew more about what was going on than all the diplomats around her dinner table combined. She had firsthand knowledge of how far the hatred had progressed.

What was the time? Settled on his subtropical café terrace, Oscar whiled the afternoon away. Time had little meaning there, the siesta canceled out all sense of urgency. He was easily drawn into the slow rhythm of a Portuguese day. He settled the bill and strolled to the tram stop. The Alfama was waking from a deep afternoon slumber, doors were opened, there was shouting and laughter. From a radio came fado music, the pride of the nation. He was not impressed. Misjudged melancholy came to mind. He remembered an evening with Envoy Sillem and his entourage, and having to endure never-ending rounds of those mournful songs. Still, Lisbon was a breath of fresh air after Berne. The city of light with the tang of brine in the breeze, the squares with palm trees, the men with their arms around each other, the gesticulations, the women in colorful dress. And no sign of war, no threat, just a strip of land on the margin of the continent, overlooked. All over Europe the lights were going out, but not there. Portugal was a lighthouse in a darkened landscape.

The downhill ride took much longer than going up, with many more people getting off and on as the tram made its leisurely, summery way to the center.

Equally leisurely had been the cog-wheel train to Lauterb-runnen, nosing down the track toward the valley, down to the mainline station and ordinary trains, back to their ordinary lives. To the parting of their ways. He sat opposite Lara, his travel bag leaning against hers, which gave him the odd sensation of having achieved something. Bag nudging bag was not such a big leap from hand in hand. The thought of her clothes folded up in her luggage was pleasing in itself. Their knees touched from time to time; the compartment was small and the incline steep. They had not spoken, they had looked out of the window, seen nothing but fir trees, top-heavy with snow. In the glass Oscar caught his reflection and Lara's in the illuminated interior, their faces averted and quiet. Two days in comparison with a lifetime was nothing, two days could not amount to much.

A conductor passed nimbly from one carriage to the next. He paused a moment on an outside ledge to close the door behind him and open the one in front, an acrobat in the service of ticket inspection, stepping from one moving carriage to the next, each with its own complement of passengers with different destinations and yet all part of the same train chugging forward at a snail's pace. The war was stealing closer, though they did their best to deny it by avoiding the subject altogether.

At Lauterbrunnen, they found themselves back in the real world. Oscar saw the platform swarming with uniforms: the Swiss had mobilized a huge army. General Guisan, whose portrait hung in all the restaurants and cafés, had proclaimed that Switzerland would defend itself against any invader, whoever that might be. The man was a secret admirer of Germany, Oscar wanted nothing to do with him.

They changed trains and resumed their *tête-à-tête* for the journey to Berne. The compartments began to fill up; a haze of tobacco smoke hung in the air. Three more hours of inchoate dialogue, possibly more discreet than in the mountains, but no less intense. Along the Thunersee, where the wheels almost touched the water, she pointed to a boat quietly setting sail. Winter or no winter, unfurling chalk-white in the sun. She pointed to the normal, everyday sights, about which there was little to be said.

Afterward, he wondered whether he had said too much about himself. He had even told her about Dick, the brother who had left Holland years earlier, and whom he missed. His nostalgia for the days when they formed an unassailable duo—something not even Kate was aware of. Two musketeers. Covered front and back, even the flanks were protected. And so they had borne the early loss of their father, and, in the confidence of their young years, had helped to raise their mother's spirits. His brother was seventeen at the time, he a year older.

Oscar had shed his natural reserve, but he managed to avoid going into what he did for a living. Something at the Dutch legation, of no particular interest. His vagueness elicited a quizzical glance from Lara, but she had not pressed him. Why had he talked so freely with her for two entire days, why did he feel so helplessly, unconditionally attracted to her? Why indeed. It was not for you to crack the codes of your soul. Oscar had dismissed the question as soon as it presented itself.

"Would it be all right if I looked you up in Fribourg?" he had said as the train entered the station of Berne, to which she had nodded, tapping the leather box containing her binoculars: "I'll be on the lookout for you."

When he went down the platform while the train pulled away close beside him, he had seen her through the window, sitting very still, hugging the box to her chest, her eyes closed.

"The terminal, Senhor, this is the last stop." Oscar alighted from the tram and ambled across Rossio Square. Even in the late afternoon the heat was heavy. He was lost, stood still and looked around him, felt in his pockets for a city map. Any direction would do, he thought.

Chapter 9

The sound of a doorbell rang through the house. She didn't recognize it at first. Her bell never rang. Then Kate realized she had to answer it. As she approached the front door, she heard a slight shuffle of feet and someone whistling softly.

"Hello Miss," Matteous said. He sounded so timid, she felt herself melt. It was almost unbearable, that shyness of his every time he greeted her. He had actually come to her house! She had not thought he would act upon her invitation.

"Matteous! Do come in, how good to see you!" She did not wish to overwhelm him with enthusiasm, but was unable to hide her delight at his coming. She had explained how to get to Barkston Gardens, and had written the address and the telephone number on a slip of paper, just in case. The note was in his hand. He put it down in front of her and said: "I can't read, Miss, or write," as though confessing to a crime.

Kate moved it out of sight as quickly as she could, mortified by her thoughtlessness. It had never come up at the hospital, but of course he couldn't read or write, what did she expect? She found herself infected by his shyness, and for several minutes they strove to find a new balance.

"What I really want, Miss, is to be able to write a letter by myself. So I could send it to a newspaper, or a radio station. I have heard that people sometimes find their families that way."

A black boy from an African wilderness, illiterate in a world steeped in the written word. It was enough to render anyone taciturn, timid, powerless.

It dawned on her that Matteous was asking her to teach him to write. A letter that would say what he had thought and lived through during all those years. A letter explaining his life, a letter home, to his mother, Kate imagined. Writing: arranging the words so that they would say what he wanted to tell his mother, although he could hardly expect her to be able to read his letter. But somebody could read it to her. And Kate pictured his mother listening to what he had written, a letter resembling a musical score, a Congolese dance, a prayer for rain, or a song for the dead. "She won't be alive anymore, Miss, will she?" he had said the day before, making it sound halfway between a statement and a question.

Would he like something to eat or drink, she asked, for she was persuaded that he was always hungry or thirsty. She could not resist making the offer, and he said yes so as not to have to say no. "No" was a word he said with difficulty, not wishing to sound disrespectful. He was wearing an old sweater of Oscar's which she had given him, and black army pants from the hospital. Matteous had approached her with great caution, his tread as soft as if he were stalking a wild animal. So he was asking her for help: teach me to write, then I can go back home.

Kate went to the kitchen, made tea, put some homemade cookies on a plate and brought it all through on a tray to the balcony.

"Come, let's sit outside."

Two chairs and a small table were all the balcony could hold. Matteous stood waiting for Kate to take a seat, and did not sit down until she urged him to. After a while she said that, yes, she would be happy to teach him for as long as he liked, for as long as he stayed in England. Was that all right with him? And she promised him that the day would come when he would write that letter.

She had not known it was possible to weep so noiselessly. It was not weeping in the usual sense, for his face was unchanged, there even seemed to be a hint of a smile. The tears spilled from his eyes as though following a logic of their own. He did not try to check them, they ran down his cheeks in rivulets, his head held high, his hands on the armrests of his chair as he faced her. She returned his gaze, made no move to console him or take his hand. She made no gesture whatsoever that might discomfit him. She saw the young soldier, the boy in the forest, the man far from home, the wounded patient in bed. She saw the son of a mother who had disappeared.

Events he had only touched upon in the past now came out in the open, in fits and starts.

"Suddenly they were there, Miss, they stormed into the houses and killed everybody they could find. My father shouted for me to run away into the forest. 'Don't look back, Matteous, don't look back,' he said. I ran, but I also looked back, and then I saw him standing there, surrounded by men raising their axes against him."

He had joined a band of children roaming the forest, in flight from their village and what had taken place there. He might have been seven years old. He had forgotten a lot, the worst had been washed away. He did not know how he had ended up in Élisabethville. Who had helped him, who gave him food, how he came out of that forest alive—it was all a great gap in his memory. He took huge leaps across time: at one moment he was seven, at the next seventeen, now he was playing in his village, now in the dancing halls of the city. Élisabethville. The way he said the name gave it something equivocal: there was wistfulness, and also a hint of a shudder, at least to a sensitive ear. To Kate's ear. She heard everything. He had never spoken in this way before. Between nostalgia and horror, in bits and pieces, a story that had neither end nor beginning. He floundered, broke off, began again. His childhood, his years in the copper mines of Élisabethville, the daylight that he only saw on Sundays. He had done what everybody did: kept his head down. They were years of hardening the heart, and of denial. Years of slow preparation for—well, for what? Matteous groped for the words. And what he had been unable to say yesterday now poured out of him all of its own. That saving the officer's life had not been a question of courage, but more one of despair. He thought he would run into a knife, or a gun, or a bayonet, get killed in action. He had nobody left anyway, they were all dead and gone. And when the bullets hit him he had almost been glad. His time had come, all would be forgotten. Hoisting the officer over his shoulder had not been hard, he had carried the man as a father would his child. Run, Matteous, don't look back, go and hide in the impenetrable forest, in the darkness where nothing is.

But he had pulled through it all, willy-nilly. The Belgian officer, the strange white man with his gloves and his watch and his good shoes, had thanked him and vowed that his rescuer in turn should survive. Matteous had laid him carefully on the ground before collapsing at his side, overcome with pain. That was how they had been borne away, side by side on narrow stretchers, beyond the range of the enemy, beyond the range of death at any rate. He had not set eyes on the white man again.

He had been shipped to London for reasons he did not understand. The Belgian government-in-exile would take care of him, he was told. But that government was not his, it had nothing to do with him. He had drifted from Africa to Europe on tides of randomness, just as he had been sucked into the advance northwards, with an army of strangers set to fight another army of strangers.

Matteous lapsed at last into silence, his eyes fixed on Kate. She had not understood everything, but she had heard his story, told in the language unique to him, complete with gestures and stammerings and bits of words.

In the street beneath them life went on as usual with its everyday sounds, with sunshine and the screech of gulls high above the buildings. He touched the sleeve of her cardigan, pressed her arm. Kate had a strange sensation of blankness in her head, could feel the blood rising to her cheeks. It was as if somewhere far away, in the unconscionable depths of her being, parcels were being unwrapped, mysterious envelopes torn open, stacks of papers riffled through. Why was it just as if Roy was sitting there, clasping her arm? Roy, who had been dead for so long, and buried in a bottomless pit. The Roy of all those mornings on their balcony in Rome, just off the Corso.

"I've sat down, Kate, come join me." The invariable invitation. Ten o'clock in the morning, church bells ringing out all around them, a fraction off synchrony. Always lovely weather, always together. In his arms, beneath him, on his knee, his hands in hers, his body in complete abandon. Nothing lasts, nothing stays the same, nothing is lost. Where had they been that last time? She thought it was the Caffè Greco, the café which had become too highly recommended in the guidebooks, but which was largely unspoiled in their day. They had stopped there on their walk to the railway station. He would be away for a couple of days, she would not accompany him. The café was all but deserted at this early hour. They chose a two-seat banquette upholstered in purple velvet, the cardinal among café furniture. A clutter of small tables, mirrors, paintings, chairs, created an obstacle course for the waiters. Their evenings in Caffè Greco, when it was packed with people, all Italians, all discussions and laughter and gesticulations, how Roy and she loved going there.

The heat had been intense that morning, the ceiling fan whirring to little effect. They had sat there as though it were the train compartment in which Roy would soon depart, first class. Kate held both her hands clasped around his upper arm, as she often did. To him the most endearing of her gestures. They had said little, just stared into the heat, idly aware of the people trickling in. Roy had stroked her hair. There was nothing in the least unusual or untoward, they were in ample time for Roy's train, just two days and he would be back with her again. From Rome to Milan and back. He was to address "a bunch of diggers" on recent developments at the Forum excavations, and he also had an appointment with a Dutch journalist whose name escaped him, but whom he would see in his hotel.

Thus their hour in the café had passed, after which they resumed their walk, holding hands probably, to the Stazione Termini, where a porter had taken charge of his bag. Had she accompanied him down the platform? She thought not. She disliked waving goodbye on platforms. There had been no high-flown words on parting—why would there be? Just a kiss on her mouth.

Suddenly, Kate felt the pressure of his hand on her arm. Matteous.

Chapter 10

They were flying at night, which was not normal practice. Neutral airlines flew during daylight hours, out in the open, so the Luftwaffe would not mistake them for the enemy. The sun was rising as they prepared for landing on the airfield at Bristol. Oscar was asleep. He was jolted awake as the wheels of the aircraft hit the tarmac. That had never happened to him on a plane before. His nerves jangled. First he would call Morton, he thought, then go to Kate's apartment. He wanted to surprise her.

Bristol, 6 a.m., Whitchurch Airport. The hands of the giant clock in the arrivals hall stood as stiffly to attention as the guards at Buckingham Palace. Oscar had plenty of time. He took the train to Paddington. Morton was expecting him, but there was no point in presenting himself at the ministry before nine. He did not really want to go there at all; he would ask Morton to meet him elsewhere. He closed the narrow door of his compartment. In England he always had the feeling of traveling on a private train, as if yours was the only compartment behind the engine. There was no corridor, no door to the adjoining compartment, no ticket collector. Ten people in a plush-lined box, a chocolate box on wheels. The first train of the day was still fairly empty, and the only other person in the compartment was a young soldier sitting by the window. Beside him was a large duffel bag with his army coat draped over it. Oscar saw two closed eyes in a pale, unshaven face. A desolate sight. Everything was desolate: the dark roof of the station, the slow tread of the stationmaster, the blurred, metallic loudspeaker announcing departure. Oscar saw a few latecomers running along the platform and leaping onto the train.

Lately he had spent more time traveling on trains than ever before. Since their days in the mountains he had seen Lara several times, taking turns to meet at his home in Berne and at hers in Fribourg. The first time was a week after they had separated. He picked her up at the station in Berne. How were her binoculars, he wanted to know.

"Idle, sitting on their ledge by the window," was her prompt reply.

To see her again—since their departure from the Oberland he had been able to think of very little else. In Berne, too, the snow was piled high in the streets, but it was nothing compared to their village up the mountain. Oscar took her to Della Casa, an inconspicuous restaurant in the Schauplatzgasse within walking distance of the station. He had lunch there sometimes with Swiss contacts, it was "spy-proof," and unknown to German agents, apparently. The proprietor was a "good" Swiss.

"Herr Verschuur, welcome! It has been a while since you were here last—how good to see you." The waiter's warmth was sincere. He bowed to Lara, took her coat and Oscar's, and led them to a table in a separate angle by the Russian stove. From the kitchen in the back came the rattle of pans and crockery. The small dining room was still empty of clients, but would soon fill up, and by two o'clock they would all be gone again. Rhythms of peacetime.

At first, all he could do was look at her. She did not seem to mind this, it was as though she understood. She said as little as he did. Oscar and Lara, in the glassy quiet of their niche.

She allowed him to observe her. He found her breathtaking, of a beauty so new to him that it was almost frightening. In the sequestered world of the mountain village he had been less conscious of it than here, on a weekday in the city. That she had made the journey especially to meet him, that she wanted to see him again, that she had taken the train, put lipstick on, ironed her blouse, glanced in the mirror before she left—unbelievable. He floundered for words.

"I was up in the mountains every day." Oscar's voice was hesitant and low, as though afraid of being overheard. "Doing all the walks in my head that we would have done had we stayed."

"I was there too. I followed you from the terrace, but you were impossible to catch up with, a bit like those chamois."

They had left the Jungfrau behind unscathed, the village had not been cut off. Unscathed? Ha, anything but. In their minds they had been cleaved together. They resumed their oblique declarations of love.

At half past twelve the regulars started to drift in, long-time patrons whom the waiter dispersed across the homely dining area with practiced efficiency. Soon all the tables were occupied, and the air was alive with the gurgles of Swiss German. The conviviality that prevailed, the effusive waiter, the sensible eaters, the bountifulness and contentment—Oscar saw and heard it all, yet he was hearing other things: sirens over London, sirens over Berlin.

He told Lara about his eternal struggle with the feeling of being in one place and simultaneously in another. Being able to talk with her, and at the same time with someone else, his daughter Emma for instance. Lara nodded. Not-quite-blue was the color of her eyes, or rather a soft green, the shade of the earliest spring. In Café Eiger they had been bluer; here in the city they were more green. Here everything about her was a shade different from the way it had been in the mountains. Ski pants, sweaters, jackets and gloves, they had been nothing but camouflage, disguise.

Those few hours in the Berne restaurant had passed strangely. From half past eleven until two, when they both had to get back to work. The next day he could not remember whether he had said anything to her that made sense. And Lara had said little. The opening skirmishes with a few poignant remarks had led to a timid exchange of questions and answers, after which a hush had fallen, a mime show in which every movement counted. The least utterance seemed out of place. Even the waiter stayed in the background, observing silence as he served them. At length Lara laid her hand next to her plate, palm up, and they both knew it was time to go. He covered her hand with his, carefully, overwhelmed by the occasion they had created for themselves. The long-deferred touch. His heart pounded, he saw the pulse throbbing at her wrist.

The pale soldier opened his eyes. Oscar, sitting diagonally opposite, nodded a greeting. The boy looked outside. The stretch between Bristol and London was familiar to Oscar from the time he visited veterans at their homes as part of the research for his thesis. Veterans from a silent film, survivors of a war that had long been forgotten and long since overlaid by new wars. The boy in his uniform had been drafted in to an age-old system: the call to arms. But he was probably thinking only of his sweetheart, or his parents, or having had to get up at the crack of dawn. Involuntarily, Oscar flicked through the history books stored in his brain. No matter where you lived, they came to get you, young as you were, strong and unafraid. Asia, Africa, Europe, here we come, we will attack, we will not give up. The tragic propensity to interfere, to bring succor, to conquer, to rule. Arrogance was an alcohol brewed in the bosom of families, in churches and schools and clubs. If there was a God, He would have to speak English to make Himself understood, and to give orders. But God seemed a very long way away.

"Right now we need Churchill more than God," Morton had said during their last encounter. "We call it practical Christianity." They had met briefly at Morton's club in August '39, when Oscar and Kate were looking for somewhere for her to live in London.

From Bristol to London, at each modest little station on the way more passengers took seats in the compartment. Amid the smoke, rustling newspapers, coughs, women's voices, Oscar and the soldier were absorbed into a run-of-the-mill English morning.

At Paddington Station he called Morton at his ministry: they arranged to meet for coffee at the Travelers Club at Pall Mall. Morton could spare him one hour.

It was raining. Did it ever stop? The rainy season here seemed to go on for twelve months of the year. After the heat of Portugal he was unprepared for this. He shivered in his summer jacket, and had come without a hat, at usual. Shouldn't he give Kate a call, let her know he was in London? But she was probably at her hospital by now, no point in disturbing her. He would simply go to Barkston Gardens and wait for her there. "Everything's fine with Emma, don't worry," he would start off by saying, to avoid undue alarm. Thinking ahead came automatically to him, forewarning, assuring that everything was all right. But it was not all right. Everything was a shambles, it was impossible to think straight. Shortly before his departure he had called Lara and told her he had to go to London, there was a meeting he had to attend. He was aware that he did not sound convincing.

"Isn't that rather sudden? Take care."

He wished he could hop on the train to Fribourg. Take care, look ahead, then you'll see me and I'll see you. A medley of anticipation. Take care. Her voice had been like an embrace.

"Mr. Morton is in the garden room. Please follow me."

Oscar knew the Travelers from the days before he knew Morton. It was a club for diplomats and politicians, established more than a century ago, and of a growth that had kept pace with that of the British Empire. Whitehall not far away, the departments within lunching distance. From the garden room you could see trees and a well-kept lawn, beyond which you knew St. James's Square to be. War or no war, the Travelers served coffee and port at all hours. He entered to find a fire burning in the hearth, the shaded lamps lit, and Morton sitting with his back to the door, sticking his hand up at the sound of approaching footsteps.

"Welcome, Verschuur."

"Good to see you, Morton."

Silence.

Morton was a man of few words, a man with a strange fire in his belly. A musketeer. Oscar could tell. It was as if Dick were sitting there, in another guise. His brother, with whom he had lived day in day out until he met Kate. Oscar had existed in the lee of their friendship, where everything went without saying. One day they had divided the world between them, laughing uproariously, with Dick claiming the women and he the poets and philosophers. But it had been Dick who had set out on his own to the East Indies with a trunk full of books. His brilliant, illusion-less brother. Their coffee was served. A small party of men were seated in a far corner, conversing in subdued voices. Through the high windows he saw people strolling past, and he could barely take it all in, the insouciance, the unspeakable complacency of his surroundings, the unperturbed demeanor of the passers-by, the delicate hand-gestures of the staff, Morton's genial greeting. Annoyance welled up in him at London's arrogant display of liberty, though it subsided the moment they embarked on their conversation larded with digressions, begged questions, snippets of news of mutual friends, of Wapenaar, of the situation in Berlin. Oscar spoke with the handbrake on, trying to ascertain how much Morton might or might not know. He described the evening at Henderson's, mentioning that Howard Smith had been present. Morton was keen to hear about Berlin, and about Smith in particular. He asked after Kelly in a conspiratorial tone, and was both surprised and pleased to hear of the Turkish envoy's involvement. Morton liked things to be raised to the level of intrigue.

The pressure mounted in Oscar's head. Slowly but surely Morton was fencing him in, inching his way forward to discover the real reason behind this sudden visit to London, reminding him that it was he, Morton, he was talking to, Morton, Churchill's personal friend and adviser. What was it all about, what was Verschuur up to?

"So Smith mentioned troop concentrations, did he?"

Oscar confirmed, adding that Smith seemed to think Russia could be attacked at any moment. This was it: now was the time to tell him. He glanced around. The group of men sitting by the fire were safely out of earshot. A waiter stood in the doorway like a sentry.

He had gone over every contingency, every coincidence, every sign, suspicion, probability, every ulterior motive, trap, deception. Every single step he might be obliged to take had been plotted, each potential countermove examined. A tangle of possibilities and impossibilities crowded his mind. If he did tell Morton, how could he ever be sure that the information would not be traced back to him? Morton would promise not to name his source, but still, he was bound to inform his agents in Berlin that he had heard, via Switzerland . . . In his ratiocinations Oscar kept coming back to himself as the only possible source. And from him to Emma, the horse's mouth. Emma was in danger, she had been seen with him in Geneva, he was under suspicion and therefore so was she, as was Carl—doubly so, because they already suspected Trott, his boss. Their meeting would have been reported back to Berlin, there was no doubt about that. Emma or Barbarossa. It had driven him mad, the despair, the rage, the unutterable sadness. There was no way of reaching Emma and Carl, no question of conferring, suggesting, advising, let alone of warning. Berlin was riddled with listening devices.

"How are your daughter and your son-in-law?"

Oscar heard the question, wanted to evade it, but said: "I saw them last week, in Geneva. We had lunch in a restaurant."

Morton glanced up. Oscar sat very still, poised to take the plunge.

"Any news from that front, by any chance?"

They would arrest Emma at their leisure, just her, not Carl. And would interrogate her at their leisure, let her stew, week after week, they would foist her onto some other interrogation team if it suited them.

"Trott wants to liaise with you. He's doing a lot to mobilize opposition to his bosses."

"We are aware of that, Verschuur, but we don't trust him. We have the impression that he's playing a double game, although we also believe that it won't be long before they invade the Soviet Union. Did your son-in-law have anything to say on the subject?"

They might let her go after a few months, but on the other hand they might very well keep her locked up indefinitely.

And then it hit him what Morton had just said: they had doubts about Trott. In other words, anything Oscar told them about Operation Barbarossa and when it was due would not be credited. His information came from Carl, and by extension from Trott, whom they did not trust. Wasn't that what Morton had said? Trott, Carl, Emma, nothing coming from them would be listened to, everybody in Germany was tainted, good Germans simply did not exist. However high the risks being taken, however brave it was to resist, the English saw nothing but duplicity. At best they were opportunists, Trott and his friends. My daughter is one of them, Morton. The message was clear: total cynicism regarding whatever forms of resistance might be striving to emerge in the land of the enemy. Oh my God, Emma.

"No, not really. Carl mentioned the west, but not the east. Smith did, explicitly so. Not Carl, though."

Morton waited, in vain. Oscar would keep the news to himself, they would not believe him anyway. The operation would go ahead, as the Russians were bound to have discovered by now. How many million troops did they count on going over there, how much murder and manslaughter could a nation endure, who would warn the people at the border, tell them to run, flee, make themselves scarce.

They fell silent, the hour was up. Morton had work to do. Mission unaccomplished.

Their footsteps on the marble floor sounded refined, their shoes creaked, their coats were held out for them, Morton's umbrella snapped open. Oscar followed him with his eyes as he picked his way between the other umbrellas in the direction of the park. The gait of a man of purpose, a man without a daughter.

Morton must have noticed that Oscar was being evasive, or even disingenuous—saying nothing can amount to lying, saying nothing can mislead. But Morton had failed to register Oscar's horror at the casual passing of the death sentence on every German, every man or woman valiantly swimming against the current.

Emma was on the wrong side, and that was that.

Chapter 11

Should she ask Adriaan Wapenaar for help? Her father had repeatedly impressed upon her to appeal to him if necessary. Emma had waved aside his concern, but had not forgotten his advice. She knew where he lived: in Grunewald, a fifteen-minute bike ride at most. There was something of the reservation about Grunewald, with its abundant greenery and here and there a tennis court between the houses. The thwack of a tennis ball among the trees epitomized the total disregard for what was happening elsewhere. Why the place had not been plundered was anyone's guess. But for some reason they had left it alone, their clubs and claw-hammers being put to use elsewhere.

She wheeled out her bicycle, nerves jangling. Why she wanted to speak to him she was not sure—just to be with another Dutch person, perhaps, to speak her own language, see a friend of her father's. She had no need of a coat; it was still early, but the warmth of June was already thick among the trees. Would Wapenaar know who she was, she wondered. They had met only twice before, and briefly at that. She took the lanes of Dahlem, crossed the main road and turned left into Grunewald. Oak trees and chestnuts caught the sun.

She pedaled along gently rolling avenues in deep shade, with bends that seemed random and illogical. The houses stood some distance apart, secluding ill-gotten gains in tranquility. Prinz-Albrecht-Strasse was only a few miles away, while here men and women sat idly in the windows, languid from the onslaught of summer. Gardeners shifted their ladders from one tree to the next. Cycling through the oasis was a journey to another planet.

Emma knew the way. She and Carl often went there, walking or on their bikes, in an optimistic endeavor to shake off the war. Carl had told her about the history of Grunewald and all the artists, writers and rich folk who used to live there. The current residents, mostly party bosses and industrialists, were an unenviable bunch, according to him. Carl Regendorf was a man without grudges of any kind, a greater contrast with the prevailing mood was impossible to imagine. Emma and Carl had fallen in love at great speed, as though intent on staying ahead of the times they were obliged to inhabit, the times of rancor and revenge and unending acts of hatred.

Birds sang in the trees. Loving him more than she did there, at that moment, was impossible to imagine. The thought played on her mind to the slow rhythm of her feet on the pedals. If only she could leave, take him with her to some other country. Their short stay in Switzerland had been so blissfully peaceful. It was there, during a stroll in Geneva, that she had said, on a sudden impulse, why don't we stay here, Carl, why go back to doom-laden Berlin? Now was the moment, this was their chance, they could disappear—her father would certainly help them. London, America, anything was better than staying put and having to watch as ruination drew near. But she knew the answer. Carl understood how she felt, naturally, but there were his parents to think of, and the rest of the family.

They would be rounded up immediately and sent to a camp, or worse. Emma abandoned the thought. They were hostages, she knew that by now.

With one hand she held the shoulder strap of her bag, a girl on her way to school, or to her grandmother's, in the filtered light of morning. She pushed the pedals around, then lifted her feet off them to freewheel almost to a standstill before pedaling onward again. She took her time cycling to Wapenaar's home in the heart of Grunewald. No hurry, as she didn't quite know what she would do when she got there. And anyway it was all a bit pointless, because there was no way she could speak her mind. Nonetheless, she pedaled on, steering her bike to the Bismarckbrücke near the Hubertus lake. She knew the address, although she had never visited the house before.

It was a small villa, not much larger than where Carl and she lived, but with a long garden reaching down to the lake. A wrought-iron gate with climbing roses gave the Wapenaar residence a romantic touch. The front entrance, too, was framed with roses.

The door was opened by a woman. Emma introduced herself, saying she was Dutch and that her father was a friend of Mr. Wapenaar's, that she happened to be cycling around in the neighborhood, and had wondered if it was all right for her to drop by to say hello. Emma's flustered preamble made the woman laugh, and she invited her in. Her husband was not at home, but that was of no consequence, she was expecting him back any minute. Would Emma like something to drink? She suggested going out into the garden to sit on the terrace by the lake with a glass of orange juice. She spoke Dutch with a strong German accent, which had a surprising charm to it. Emma did not have the nerve to decline the hospitable offer, and meekly followed Wapenaar's wife into the garden. It was eleven o'clock, the lake at their feet was smooth and black. A dog barked in the next garden. It seemed unreal, a scene in a film. What was she doing there, why had she come?

The dog carried on barking, growling, yelping, running and jumping up against an invisible fence alarmingly close by. Wapenaar's wife went over and called the animal by its name, softly and commandingly, then put her hand through the hedge to pat it. Order was restored, quiet reigned once more.

"She's a nice enough creature, but she's been left alone for far too long."

Emma nodded understandingly. Alone for far too long, that was something she was finding increasingly difficult to cope with. Carl going off to work, leaving her sitting at home facing a lonely, empty day ahead of her and having to find things to keep her busy until he came home in the evening. Days during which she banished the war to the back of her mind and worked in her garden, weeding and pruning. The pretense of normality was a way of dealing with a hostile environment, something she saw women everywhere attempting to do, acting as if nothing was wrong, as if they were leading their ordinary lives. Was it not ever thus for wives, whose husbands were always working, as soldiers, bakers, professors, civil servants, ministers?

Emma eyed the friendly woman over the glasses of orange juice on the table between them. There was an idyllic-seeming quality to the setting, which she was loath to disturb. The woman asked Emma to call her Elka, a nickname, really, dating from her childhood, when her father used to write little notes to her always beginning with a capital *L* and a capital *K*, for *Liebes Kind*. And so she became Elka. Emma listened, thinking that she could not remember her father ever writing little notes to her. Her father, whom she missed so achingly now, and who seemed to be drifting further and further away from her.

Since her parents moved away from Berlin she had not been back to Fasanenstrasse, where she and Carl had first met, where her unmoored existence had begun. Her courage at the outset, like her nostalgia for what she had to leave behind, had been boundless. She and Carl swam upstream, never tiring or losing hope, never afraid. After her parents' farewell dinner she had watched him as he walked away, and he had turned around and seen her, and had waved in surprise because she was waving too. That cheerful, hopeful hand still waved at her each day from the garden gate. Carl was the complete opposite of her father, as transparent as glass, a miracle of straightforwardness.

Through the open windows reverberated the chimes of a clock striking the hour. Emma counted twelve—she had been there for an hour already, she must leave. She apologized for staying so long, saying she would come back another day, if that was all right. A whole hour! She cringed with embarrassment. She had hardly said a word while Elka Wapenaar entertained her, squeezed oranges for her, rocked her to sleep, so it seemed.

She headed back to Dahlem, cycling on automatic pilot as she thought of her father. And for the umpteenth time of the remark about her mother. The glint in her interrogator's eyes had been malicious, his tone insinuating. Quite a looker, know what I mean. Do you get what I'm saying. Suddenly it dawned on her. Clamping the brakes hard, she heard the tires skid over the road. Her father had another woman.

She stopped, parked her bicycle in the verge and cast around for a bench to sit on. Her inclination was to weep, but the tears did not come. Her face was hot, her hands were cold. Quite a looker. Her thoughtless, faithless father had been seen in the company of a woman, and not just any woman. They had been followed, and even from a distance her appearance had been striking, or rather, her father had obviously found her striking. That had to be it: the mystery of his evasiveness in Geneva explained. He had been half out of his mind when he joined her and Carl, his eyes more than once shifting away from hers. Emma looked around her: it was busier now on Königsallee, with people on foot and on bicycles passing by. To her surprise, it was not plain anger that she felt, rather an old sadness. It had to do with something she had been hiding for years. That she did not really know her father. Her love for him was so naive and unconditional. As love should be. Her father, who belonged with her mother, who would never leave her, never ever, not for anybody, not even for the love of his life, or whatever she was. Suddenly she was seized with rage. Rage over what he was putting in the balance, over his bit on the side, over his secrecy and his deceitfulness and his refusal to meet her gaze.

She picked up her bike and wheeled it to the side of the road, hardly aware of where she was going, unable to stem the flood of memories.

She saw him enter the restaurant where he was meeting her and Carl. Her boyish papa. She had gone up to him as quickly as decorum permitted, she had thrown her arms around him, had taken his hand and drawn him to their table, where Carl was waiting. It had been more than a year since she had seen him, a radically altered world ago, countless bombing raids and massacres ago, though nothing of that was mentioned. It was too much, too overwhelming, too huge to grasp. She had watched him and seen the shadows passing across his face, the way he sidetracked her as soon as she asked him a personal question, the way he seemed not to want her to get too close. He probably hadn't even wanted to be there at all, she could see that now. He had been at pains to avoid every form of intimacy. Had he taken against her marriage with Carl? No, that was unlikely, as she could tell he regarded Carl as a friend. He had even spent more time talking to him than to her.

"The last time we were together, you, me and Mama, was up here in the mountains, wasn't it?" His discomfort had become almost palpable when she said that. He responded by asking her about Berlin, steering the conversation away from himself yet again. Her feelings had been hurt, she had so looked forward to this, longing to see him, hear him, relish the known gestures, be close.

Another woman, for God's sake, Papa. Her rage flared up again, at him, and at the Gestapo for exposing him. What were they after, why would they be so interested in him? Her father, with a lock on his mouth and a lid on his soul. What else had he been up to all these years?

From nearby came the sound of those wretched tennis balls; playing tennis now was a criminal pastime, a cruel joke. She would leave Carl out of it, much as she ached to confide in him. In some ways she resembled her father, she realized. She would keep this to herself.

"Looking for someone?" A man on a bicycle slowed down, stopped, and looked her up and down. She shook her head and prepared to move on.

"Your papers, please." The condescending tone of an informer, or at any rate of a party member sporting a fancy badge. He probably lived somewhere nearby. But this was beyond the pale. Emma struggled to keep her voice under control.

"Yes indeed, I do have papers. But I am not going to show them to you. And if you don't leave me alone immediately I shall file a complaint at my husband's department."

Her voice rose as her anger mounted. It was an impulsive, irrational outburst, but no less effective for that. The man stiffened, mumbled an apology and sped away on his bicycle.

Emma lapsed into nervous laughter as she stood there in a world gone insane, where people demanded to see each other's papers.

Chapter 12

Kate took the bus to Richmond Hospital in the morning as usual, to return in the afternoon. The Richmond was a repository of the sick and wounded from ever farther corners of the earth, a round-the-clock enterprise. She liked her job. The patients followed one another in rapid succession, and she had a knack for putting people at ease and seeing to their wants and needs with discretion. "Head of subtle affairs," one of the doctors called her, a man who reminded her vaguely of Peter Henning, the surgeon she had worked with for over a year in Berlin, at a time when murder and manslaughter were already the order of the day. He had fallen in love with her, she not with him, but it had lightened the atmosphere in and around the operating theater. Oscar was unaware of this, and there was no reason to worry him unduly. That was all of five years ago.

Kate saw the traffic on her bus route increase. It started to rain, and London unfurled its umbrellas. For no particular reason her mind turned to the time she had gone to the stadium with Peter. The Olympic Games had transformed the city, making it brighter and cleaner than ever before. He had invited her to accompany him to the athletics competitions taking place that afternoon. They had finished work early, no further surgery being required for the day.

They drove through a city on temporary reprieve from the grip of steel. Peter, being a doctor, had a car, enabling them to reach the Olympic stadium without difficulty. Across Tiergarten to Charlottenburg they went, where the flags would have been enough to festoon the Kurfürstendamm from end to end. Kate recalled how Peter always gave his car a pat on the hood before he got in: good dog. It was a Mercedes with a canvas hood, one of those wonderful sleek jobs with big headlights and a running board, the very ones she had, in time, grown to despise. There always seemed to be men in leather coats with wide belts getting out of them. Peter was not someone who associated with those types; he was the last likable German she had met, aside from Carl, of course.

He had put his arm around her shoulder when they entered the stadium. She had not objected. To her his warm personality was endearing, and the way he held her had nothing possessive about it, having more of boys on their way to a game of football and out to have a good time. His left hand rested near her neck, with his right he fought to keep the umbrella positioned over her head in the multitude thronging to see the games. He had brought her up to date on the various events: discus, high jump and javelin. The names of the athletes meant nothing to her, but she was carried away by his enthusiasm, wanting to know if there were any Dutch participants and which ones to look out for. She pointed up to his umbrella, saying the rain had stopped. He laughed, and removed his hand from her shoulder, which she thought a pity in a way, as it had given her a sense of togetherness, of being part of the crowd milling around them, where no one knew her, where they were just another couple lining up to take their seats on a stadium bench. Her pleasure had nothing to do with the man beside her, charming as he was, glancing at her and gallantly removing his coat so she could sit on it.

Where would Peter Henning be now? Kate sat by the window of her bus, thinking how odd it was that her memory of that afternoon should be so vivid. Afterward, they had gone to the bar of Hotel Esplanade, where she thought Oscar might be, and he was. They had spent the evening there, with Peter and Oscar in animated conversation. Athletes and results were hotly debated in the smoke-filled bar, which was crowded with foreigners, Olympic officials, and reporters. Berlin had never felt freer or more exuberant. Peter had insisted on dropping them off at home, Fasanenstrasse being too far away for them to walk. He had lowered the canvas hood of the car; it was a warm evening. Besides, the rain had stopped, he said, flashing her a smile. Upon arrival he held the car door open for her and helped her alight, squeezed her hand briefly, saying he had enjoyed their outing immensely and would never forget it. Oscar had joined them as they stood there, putting one arm around her and the other around Peter. An August evening as never before. She would not forget it either.

The bus pulled up, she had to get off.

Peter had left the hospital a few months later. Kate had received a letter from him explaining his motives in the vaguest of terms. She had found it very strange, they had made such a good team in the operating theater. Had he fled, was he Jewish by any chance? Was it something to do with her? That was the last she had heard of him. Shortly after that she had resigned as well.

In the hall of the Richmond she found herself in a crush of people. Not far away a bomb had exploded, one of those that went off by accident, days or weeks after being dropped. By accident indeed, for today there were dozens of wounded and several dead. A frequent occurrence, but no less harrowing for that. There were dormant bombs all over the city.

Kate took the stairs to her wing. She paused a moment before entering the ward, listening to the moans of the wounded down in the hall. It was not for her to offer first aid as she was no longer a nurse, and would not even be permitted to help. Nobody knew that she had worked as a theater assistant in Berlin, and she had preferred to keep things that way. In a few days' time some of those wounded would turn up in her ward anyway: more cases for the subtle affairs department. Kate wanted to deny it, but failed: now that Matteous had been discharged, the hospital seemed to have lost its spirit. She had a sense of vacancy, in a ward brimming with need. The cubicle she had visited daily for so many months had a new occupant, equally injured and equally in need of assistance. So yes, she would step in, but she was already looking forward to the afternoon, when she would teach Matteous to write.

He would be arriving in an hour, armed with the tools for the letter he would write one day: copybook, pen, and primer. They had been practicing every afternoon for a whole week. The alphabet had been recited and painstakingly written out. Kate had pronounced each letter in a clear, slow voice, over and over again. Matteous wanted to write in English, the language he had first heard in the mines of Élisabethville. She had no idea how to teach somebody to read and write. She could not remember how she had been taught herself. You had a picture alphabet, you had Jack and Jill going up the hill—how on earth did these things go? You were a sponge absorbing words which you then squeezed out onto the page; five or six years old, the magical age of seeing letters turn into words. Had there been any particular method to it? She did not know, she would simply go on teaching Matteous the basics of English as best she could.

The small table by the window was their practice field. They sat side by side for many a long hour, with Matteous hunched over a word taking shape under his pen, even as it fell apart again. They repeated the sounds countless times, looking to see how they fluttered down onto the paper. Kate gave the example and Matteous followed suit with ink-stained fingers. He became agitated, repeatedly getting stalled halfway through what he wanted to say, the simplest of statements coming out garbled. Coherence was what was lacking. There were all those letters strung into words, which, taken together, did not make sense. It drove Matteous to distraction. He would rather be trudging through the forest, going down the mines, even marching through the savannah with a gun over his shoulder—anything was better than this blind grappling with script. Kate understood. She too found it hard to stay the course. But she had given him her word, and would not go back on it now.

She also understood how stifled he must feel at Barkston Gardens, confined as he was to a classroom of a few square yards overlooking a garden with a fence around it. He had traveled thousands of miles only to end up here, in the home of a white woman who made him acutely aware of the loss of his mother. Too bad then, forget about writing a letter, he would simply go back to Élisabethville, where else was there to go? Living in a studio on a busy London street would be the end of him. It was a week since he had moved in, and already his head was bursting. The dreams he had at night were wearing him out, he could hardly get out of bed in the morning. It was only the thought of seeing Miss Kate that kept him going, he had told her in a roundabout way.

This afternoon he was early. Kate saw him from the window. The rain had stopped. He was wearing an old army shirt, no jacket or sweater. A Negro. People noticed him, some stared. The gardener paused in his labors to call out to Matteous, she could not make out what. The bell rang, two short bursts in rapid succession, and she flew to the door. But at the third word he tried to write he put his pen down and slumped forward, head down on the table. His eyes were closed: this was no act of protest, it was defeat. He was stumped, the thoughts arising in his head were impossible to cram into words on paper. Miss Kate should let him go, he wanted to go home, not that he knew where that was, because Élisabethville was an empty place and his village had been razed to the ground. It was true that the Belgian officer had saved his life, but if it hadn't been for Miss Kate he would have been found with a rope around his neck long ago. Would she please let him go, please, Miss Kate, s'il vous plaît.

Kate stared at the curls on Matteous's dark nape as she listened to his lament. She heard his sorrow and his homesickness and his confusion. Nobody could learn to write in a single week; it might be a year before that letter of his was ready to be sent, the letter that would restore his life to him; it was too soon to give up, and why go back now, not knowing who or what awaited him there? He could come live with her until the war was over. And they would go on practicing until he couldn't get it wrong, he would master the skill, that much was certain.

She laid her hand on his shoulder as a promise. Kate's eyes, too, were closed. And so they shared a moment of darkness as they sat at the table.

Chapter 13

Somewhere in the back of her mind she heard footsteps in the stairwell, then the sound of a key turning in a lock. Was that her front door? Matteous had just left, promising to return the following day. Hardly had she relinquished her musings than she saw him. Oscar. She was thrown into confusion to find him standing in her room, then fear struck as she thought of Emma. She grabbed him by the arms. What was the matter, why hadn't he said he was coming to London?

"Emma is fine. It's Operation Barbarossa, they're going to invade Russia, Kate, in just over a fortnight from now." Oscar's tone was brusque. Her bewilderment grew by the second, what was he talking about, how did he know, what was he doing in London anyway? A curious anger overcame her. She should have been glad to see him, but his sudden appearance had the opposite effect. Invade? It was he who had invaded her home—Operation Barkston Gardens.

She found herself resenting the fact that Oscar had let himself in with his own key. For the past eighteen months she had been living there on her own, and his arrival had broken the magic circle she had drawn around herself, shattering her hard-won equilibrium.

The doors to the balcony were open. Oscar could smell the warm, damp weather that had been forecast on the radio. He was leaning in the doorway to the balcony. That she should be annoyed by his surprise visit was the last thing he expected. She had gone to her bedroom, saying she needed to change out of her hospital clothes. An excuse, he thought: she wanted to compose herself, did not wish him to see her upset.

What he had failed to tell Morton or anyone else, he had told her without a moment's hesitation. The information which had obsessed him for the past week, which he had agonized over day and night without reaching any conclusion, was safe with Kate. Her reaction would be the same as his, she would do the same, she would accept his judgment and understand and tell him it was all right and to stop tormenting himself.

Kate's face was pale. She did not look at Oscar when she joined him by the door to the balcony. She strove to control her emotions; he saw her pursed lips.

"You must inform the English, Oscar, or our government, or the people who need to know such things. You know who they are."

She spoke in measured tones, plainly, with utter conviction that it would be the simplest, most obvious action to take.

"But they will make the connection with Emma. We were seen together in Geneva, I can't tell anybody, it's impossible. This morning I had a meeting with the only Englishman I could conceivably take into my confidence, because I trust him. But I discovered that he and all his friends in high places will not believe me, whatever I say. News from a German source is by definition a lie, dismissed as nonsense. Anything coming from Berlin is regarded as disinformation. They're suspicious in the extreme. You can be sure that they'd go and check what I heard from Carl, just in case, which will not escape the notice of the Gestapo. Next thing, they'd be on to Emma."

Kate nodded. "I understand what you're saying and I'm thinking about it, but to me it sounds rather far-fetched. If Emma is at all at risk, then it's because she's your daughter, Oscar. I'm sure they suspect you of all sorts of things, they're not having you followed for nothing. Do you suppose they know about the refugees?"

Like Oscar, she never discussed his work, but one day he had let slip that he was involved in helping victims of persecution. She had given her blessing at once. Despite his secretive nature, she was aware of his ideals and his strongly developed sense of justice. She suspected that what he was doing meant taking considerable risks, which he would have dismissed as nothing compared to the risk of living in London. She had never really known what went through his mind, perhaps she had not made enough effort to work it out. It seldom gave her pause, nowadays. Under the same roof or a couple of countries away, it amounted to much the same thing, there was the same distance between them. She had the idea that his brother was probably the only person Oscar had ever opened up to. But his brother was absent. Vanished, in other words, he had emigrated to escape the Depression and the war, which he had seen coming. They had heard from him sporadically over the years, but lately not at all. Oscar had given up trying to track him down. Since then he too seemed to have absented himself.

"Emma is constantly on my mind. I'm terrified each time the English attack Berlin. Did they fly over Dahlem, was she in the city by any chance, will she reach a bomb shelter in time— not a night goes by without me imagining all the things that could go wrong. No one is more concerned about her than I am. But I honestly can't imagine that she'll be put in danger if you go to the English with your news about that invasion. For heaven's sake, Oscar, do something, while there's still time."

She had misunderstood, he would start afresh, explain all over again what would happen if he sounded the alarm. How easy it would be to single him out as the source. The whole circus of diplomats and secret agents was built on gossip and hearsay, not to mention the intentional leaking of snippets of information. He was certain that his name would crop up sooner or later. There would be Russians making inquiries among German diplomats, asking about an operation code-named Barbarossa. Never heard of it, of course, whatever gave them that idea? Oh, someone in the circuit, some Dutch specialist in Berne. The Gestapo would do the rest.

The film had played countless times in his head, and with each replay the riddle of the source became easier to solve, as in a game of simultaneous chess where you knew all your opponent's moves beforehand. This was how it would go, that was where it would go wrong. Morton had been the only possibility. And Morton would not believe him, he had now discovered. Pointless, all of it.

Her concluding words had been spoken softly, but sounded almost threatening. Pathos on a balmy June evening, irrational, unthinking. She pressed on, in the same even, concentrated voice, and perhaps with the same pathos, but with trenchant effect. He had never heard her speak in that manner before. How little he had seen of her since their days in Berlin! Theirs was marriage at a distance, in every sense. Not too many questions, no arguments, no ups and downs, and yet their loyalty to one another was never an issue. Things could be a lot worse.

She told him about her life in London, the Blitz, the ever-present threat of annihilation. But at least they were prepared. They had dug themselves in, the English defenses were ready, and however scared they were, they were prepared. No one would be caught unawares. Did he realize that there were hundreds of thousands of people out there who would be caught unawares, and what that would mean? Women of Emma's age, with children, husbands, parents, they would burn to ashes. For once, Kate spoke in capital letters. She kept bringing Emma into it, she was sure that Emma knew what she was doing when she confided in her father. Emma had counted on Oscar to know what to do about the terrible secret. She was safe, she had the protection of Carl's boss and of the ministry. That was true, wasn't it? Emma would be all right. He had to do something, immediately, there was no time to lose. Her voice as she said these things was oddly quiet. Oscar did not interrupt, much as he wished to. The numbness that had come over him seemed to increase during her appeal. Because that was what it was: an appeal, on the brink of an accusation—the way she looked at him and did not see, the way she clung to his arm and did not feel. There was no judge, but there was a verdict.

"We don't trust him, Verschuur"—anything of that provenance would be brushed aside. It was wasted on Morton.

Every fiber of his being rebelled against agreeing with Kate. Clearly, she needed to put things in perspective, he was sufficiently familiar with the Gestapo to know how they inflated the flimsiest evidence into a crime.

Yet he admired her for her outright rejection of violence and her ability to empathize with nameless Russians. For her strength of character in putting her daughter in the balance. She was discounting Emma, yet she could not abide the thought of other people's daughters losing their lives. She did not know what she was saying.

As he stood beside her, his impulse was to cover her mouth with his hand, out of a tenderness he had not felt for a long time. He wanted to interrupt, prevent her voice from reaching his ears, shield Emma from her mother's powers of persuasion. Everything she was saying was true. Kate, you are right. But what you want is impossible. They won't listen, it would all be for nothing. That operation will go ahead regardless, but Emma would pay the price, believe me, I know what I'm saying. There's no stopping them, Kate, we can't save those millions of people. You can't save people who don't save themselves.

When she had said her piece she looked away, waiting for his answer.

Chapter 14

It was still daylight when they entered the Lyons Corner House. The sun had set, leaving a swathe of pink in the dark blue sky, while the barrage balloons resembled party decorations on a distant ceiling. An attack by the Luftwaffe could not have been further from people's minds. Summer filled the streets. Blackout time was not for a while yet, and from the open windows wafted the sound of voices and radio music. The illusion of a weekday like any other, the way things used to be.

Kate and Oscar said little. After their conversation on the balcony, silence had ensued. Their disagreement was total. Kate had wept, something she very rarely did, and after a long pause Oscar reiterated all he had said before. Emma stood like a ghost between them. Her name was the linchpin of their argument.

Emblazoned in his memory was the afternoon which had haunted him for so long, and which now came rushing back. It was late August, and they were taking Emma to stay with her grandparents in Leeuwarden. Kate and he were to be posted to Washington for a minimum of four years. Emma was twelve, and of an age to start secondary education. Until then she had accompanied them on various postings, which meant contending with a succession of schools. To continue in this way would not be fair on her, they decided, whereupon Kate's parents had promptly offered to have their granddaughter live with them.

Emma had kept her eyes on him, rather than on her mother. Wasn't he the one who had promised her over and over that he would take her with him wherever he went, even to the ends of the earth?

A child's wish list, a father's little white lie.

Kate had hugged her mutely, while her parents hovered in the background, equally tight-lipped. Oscar had stood there alone, facing the jury, saying they would be back on leave in a year's time, wanting to explain once more the inexplicable.

Emma had not shed a tear, nor had she waved back when he waved his hat at her from the far end of her grandparents' hallway. She had not even walked them to the door. Her refusal to return his wave had been the bitterest regret. That empty moment, the irrevocable rift between them.

The Lyons Corner House was quite crowded, but they managed to find a vacant table. The evening's fare was chalked up on an old blackboard. London appeared to have been put on rations.

"You'd think we were under siege, judging by that menu."

Kate stroked the back of his hand. Gradually, they warmed to one another again: time-honored reflexes of a long, shared life.

"Yes, as if it's your turn to eat today and mine tomorrow."

Kate laughed softly, and met his gaze at last.

"Perhaps they'll make an exception for us, so we can both order?" Their warmth rose by a few more degrees.

She asked after his daily life in Berne, which he had barely mentioned in his letters, he asked after hers, which she had not mentioned at all. She told him about the Richmond, and what she did there as "head of subtle affairs." And about the doctor who reminded her of Peter Henning.

"Peter Henning?"

"Don't you remember that night in the bar of the Esplanade Hotel, when he and I had been to the Olympic Games?"

"And you looked like a schoolgirl with her first boyfriend— of course I remember. What has become of him, do you know?"

She did not know. She was amused by Oscar's remark, and wondered whether she might have been a little bit sweet on Peter after all.

And finally she told him about Matteous. How she had visited him, tentatively, taking two steps forward and one back in cautious progression. She described Matteous in unearthly terms. Oscar imagined someone who could have been her son, a black brother to Emma. Or, stranger still, a primordial loved one, ageless, nonexistent except in her dreamed past. A selfless, undemanding love.

Kate's voice was strong and clear. Oscar listened with close attention, now and then asking a question about the boy.

"All I want is to write a letter." That was what he had said. The deepest wish of a refugee, of someone who had left home forever, only to return there in his nightmares. To write a letter. Letter-writing was so integral to Oscar's existence that the enormity of that wish took a while to sink in. A letter as a weapon against the senselessness, against the devastation, against the oblivion, a letter as a rite of exorcism, as proof of life reclaimed.

Kate said nothing. The blackout curtains had now been drawn across the tall windows of the dining hall, and the tables were lit by sparse chandeliers. Two waiters glided through the décor, bearing trays with wine-filled glasses. Rationing did not extend to wine, apparently. Oscar registered the scene. He kept having to remind himself where he was, and why he was there, and that June 22 was almost upon them.

For heaven's sake, Oscar, it's not too late. Her exasperation still rang in his ears. He was shocked by Kate's refusal to see his side of the argument, while feeling utterly disarmed by her account of Matteous.

"Do you ever think of Roy?" A loose cannon, a question out of the blue. Had he actually asked her that? He never mentioned Roy, and Kate never mentioned him either, Roy had become an irrelevance, a sunken corpse, rejected, pulverized, secreted. Where on earth did that question come from, who started this? It was against all their rules. Had she jumped to her feet and left, he would have understood, had she looked angry or sad, or ordered something from a passing waiter, or ignored him by asking a counter-question, had there been any such reaction, he would have understood. How idiotic to raise the subject now, at this hour, after so many years, when they should be discussing something so very different.

The past is never truly past, he thought.

But Kate remained seated, unfazed by Oscar's question. Her whole life had been lived within a heartbeat of the answer.

The years with Roy, they were gone, but still on permanent standby, filtered, washed clean, as light as a feather, and of an extreme, unassailable tenderness. But what of it, there was no footstep light enough to tread the filmy foundation of happiness laid back then. Oscar, you are too heavy, my base cannot support your weight. That is why I never mentioned those days; it was not for your sake, but for my own. Yes, I do think of Roy sometimes, I never stopped thinking of him. But since meeting Matteous, when I lie awake in the early hours and the world's still asleep, I've been back, back in Rome, back in his arms. That's not being unfaithful, Oscar, it's being faithful. It's because of Matteous; it has to do with a feeling that has come over me lately, an almost animal sensation of caring about another person with reckless dedication. His skin, his eyes, the way he gropes for words—they blew me away. Roy in the shape of a black boy: what an extraordinary image to conjure up in middle age. Everything from the past repeats itself, only not ever in the same form. Roy is gone, though even that is open to interpretation. He's still there, somewhere in my body. I can touch him in the small hours, or perhaps he touches me.

She was uncertain whether to answer him at all. Not one of the thoughts going through her mind would she be able to articulate.

"Yes, Oscar," she said eventually. Her tone was reassuring, affirmative as in giving him her word. "Why do you ask?"

His turn. The onset of a response just as unintended and unexpected as his question about Roy. Something he had never told her, an account he had drafted over and over in his mind, letters to her that had been shelved in his brain, the kind of letter that Matteous would presumably never write. No better camouflage for embarrassment than putting pen to paper. He felt more than embarrassed about what he had failed to tell Kate. At first he had thought to spare her feelings, but it had become increasingly difficult to broach the subject. He simply had not got around to it. Cowardice, he now thought, cowardice disguised as consideration.

"I knew Roy, Kate."

The story he could dream poured out of him in a long stream of words. He was one of the last people to have spoken with Roy, on the day before his fatal train journey back to Rome. A few hours at his hotel in Milan, third floor, room 312. From the open window came the echo of chatter in the Corso Vittorio Emanuele, the sun was shining on the Piazza del Duomo beyond. It was July 8, 1909, thirty-two years ago.

It was yesterday, when he was a reporter for *Het Vaderland*.

Thirty-two years is a long time to keep a secret. But not for Oscar, cover-up artist and dealer in old, disposable, explosive matters.

"Did you come all the way from Holland to see me?"

Roy de Winther's surprise had not been feigned.

"You have made quite a name for yourself at home—in certain circles, anyway. The articles you publish enjoy a wide readership. The newspapers write about you, and you have the esteem of your fellow archaeologists. It was the latter that piqued the interest of my editor: the appreciation shown for a colleague who is out of the country." That was roughly how they had embarked on their conversation.

The editor-in-chief had suggested in passing that the thesis Oscar was working on could be regarded as a form of archaeology, in that it consisted of digging up old men and taking down stories. "Interesting man, that de Winther, I'm told. He will be speaking at a conference in Milan. It might be an idea to go there and write a piece about him for the paper."

No further encouragement had been necessary. De Winther was his senior by eight years. Oscar had done his homework, he was aware of de Winther's publications, his reputation, his wide-ranging travels, the fact that he and his wife had lived all over Europe, and that he was currently based in Rome.

"What is your opinion of Schliemann?"

Oscar took the bull by the horns. There was still a lot of controversy surrounding the man, though he had been dead for all of twenty years.

"A shrewd treasure seeker, but with a nose for interesting locations. He was an inveterate smuggler of his own finds, but as far as Troy is concerned he was probably right."

The tone was set, much to Oscar's pleasure, and doubtless also to that of his future readers: he could already see the headline in the paper. The state of archaeological research passed in review at speed. De Winther spoke with fervor and erudition, showing no less interest in Oscar's historical studies than in the ongoing Roman Forum excavations. They had lost track of time, although de Winther had said he only had an hour and a half to spare, apologizing for his tight schedule. It was almost eight when Roy was sorry to say that time was up—there was a diggers' banquet he had to attend, and he still had to change for dinner, order a taxi, pack his bag. He would be returning to Rome in the morning.

Oscar had returned to his hotel on foot, and sat down at a seldom-used desk in the lobby to make notes of their conversation, entire passages of which he could recall verbatim. Friendship is not forged in a few hours, but from the very start he had felt a strong rapport with de Winther. They shared the same language and the same interests, including the idea of journalism as a form of archaeology, and vice versa. What was hidden had a tale to tell. The soldiers of the Battle of Isandlwana had been persuaded to break their self-imposed silence, just as the mounds of the Roman Forum were plundered to reveal their treasures. The two men had spoken with candor, and at times drifted far from their subject into their personal lives. De Winther spoke of his plans for the future, Oscar of his.

He had thought to jot down some ideas and work them out later, but had sat there writing until well past midnight. The porter had brought him tea, and afterward a glass of port. His report would not do for a newspaper article: half of it would have to be cut for being too personal, but he wanted to record everything he could remember about their encounter—his own thoughts, his reaction to Roy's theories, Roy's razor-sharp observations—all in hurried phrases and random order. Notes of a passionate interview. Oscar had the impression of having successfully captured the essence of Roy de Winther.

He had promised to run the text past de Winther prior to publication. The occasion to send it never arose. Oscar had stuffed the sheets into an envelope and had never looked at them again. He had informed his editor that, unfortunately, he had no text to submit, as the appointment with de Winther had been to look him up in Rome. It was at that time that he had embarked on the course that became his expertise over time: concealment and secrecy.

When Oscar stopped talking, when his account came to an abrupt end—the train had yet to crash, but what sense was there in going on?—a great weariness descended on him.

Kate sat stunned, as if she had just heard that her house had been burgled. Which it had, in a way. But she regained her composure, and once more stroked the back of his hand, which was now clenched into a fist.

She refrained from asking the obvious questions: why didn't you tell me when we first met, why tell me now, why wait so long, why leave something so fundamentally important to me lying somewhere in an envelope? Oscar gave the extended fingers a light squeeze. It was the most intimate gesture he was capable of.

All the tables had been cleared by now, and the waiters were giving Oscar and Kate impatient looks.

Chapter 15

The night in Kate's apartment was spent waiting for morning to arrive. No longer used to sharing a bedroom, they lay staring wide-eyed into the dark, now and then dozing off, now and then whispering "Are you asleep?" Their beds were like two small islands adrift in an uncharted ocean.

So much had been discussed and so much left unsaid that they rose exhausted. Over breakfast they sat with expressionless faces drinking their tea, each sunk in their private thoughts of the restive night. The sounds of Barkston Gardens coming awake could be heard through the balcony doors, which were open to the early sunshine.

Hardly a word was said as they made ready for Oscar's departure to Berne. He would not be seeing Matteous, whose lesson was not until late afternoon. Oscar said how sorry he was to miss him, and hoped they would meet some time later in the year.

"Stick with him, Kate, that letter of his must get written." She glared: he didn't know what he was talking about. Later that year? Would the world still exist, would their lives still fit together, would Emma and Carl be free, and the Russians, God, the Russians, what would become of them?

The morning seemed without end, just as the night before. At two o'clock it was time to go; he had a daylight flight, for a change.

Kate made one final mention of Emma and Barbarossa, and one final appeal to him. He gave her a look as if to say that she had missed the point entirely. They waved at one another from their separate islands. He waved again from the pavement outside, and went on his way. She stood on her balcony.

Like a sleepwalker, he boarded the bus, the train, the plane. Like a sleepwalker, he arrived in Lisbon, and at long last found himself in Berne. A tool in nobody's hands. Every movement he made was automatic and slow. He trailed after the people ahead of him, joined lines when required, submitted to customs checks, showed his passport to whomever it concerned. Papers, documents, where to, where from—he complied dutifully with every demand during the interminable journey home. Home to the stark vacuity of the house on Ensingerstrasse, where the mailman whistled as he made his deliveries, where children played games on the pavement and the occasional motor car drove by at a snail's pace. Where there was not the faintest intimation of the war that was all over the newspapers: Crete fallen, tank battles in Africa, planes shot down, vessels destroyed. A paper reality, abstract. It was a normal day in June.

Oscar arrived at three in the afternoon, the sleepiest, haziest hour of the day. The emptiness overwhelmed him. It was strange how the absence of anything could have such an effect. As if nothing was familiar, as if he had stepped into someone else's life, had penetrated, thief-like, into a domain that was his but stripped of value or memory. The doors and windows were closed, the table had not been cleared, the sofa was strewn with old newspapers, the clock stood still. The occupant had clearly left in great haste, whether intending to return was impossible to say.

He stood in the middle of the room still holding his travel bag, because there was no one to take it from him or say "You can leave your luggage over there."

He who tries to forget remains a prisoner, he who cares to remember feels free.

Oscar wished in particular to free himself of the memories of the past few days.

"Do you still have that envelope, Oscar?" Kate had looked away when she asked him during breakfast the next morning—couldn't resist asking, of course. Two days ago already.

"I kept it along with the notes for my thesis. In an envelope from Hotel Vita in Milan."

The cardboard box containing his thesis material had traveled with him to each of his postings, and was now in a cabinet in his study, labeled "*Milan 1909 / Thesis 1913.*" The ink had faded, the scrawl was barely legible. He had never opened the box again, but had seen it very often, confronting him balefully both in his mind's eye and from its recess in the cabinet. Roy de Winther. How could a man so brilliant die so young, a man so attractive, happy, enterprising, and successful? One careless mistake by an engine driver, one drowsy signal master's oversight.

"To live is to dream, and death, I think, is what awakens us."

A line from a poem. Oscar stood where he was, letting his mind wander. Then he set his bag on the floor, went over to the sofa, gathered the newspapers and burned them in the fireplace. Slowly, his soul returned to him. And Lara. She had been with him all along, inseparable from him in mind, locked in soundless, abstract dialogue. He would call her shortly, tell her he had arrived in Berne and would be going straight on to Fribourg. Fribourg, the name of the town sounded so free, so fresh and unfettered, so like her. This was it, there was no going back now. Love by accident, by fate, without escape or future. He wished he could have stayed with her in the snow of the Berner Oberland—which was what he had wished from the start, a little over three months ago. From Berne to Fribourg was a stone's throw, so why not pick up his bag and go?

He had no answer. He left the bag where it stood, and stretched out on the sofa. Dog-tired he was, his legs leaden, even lying down made him ache. The machine ground to a halt. He dozed, though not for long. A dream jolted him awake, something to do with his mother. His first impulse was to call her. Old habits—his mother had been dead for a good five years. She had died with the illusion that peace could be maintained, having kept her war resister's brooch with the broken rifle like a crucifix on her bedside table, next to the photograph of his father, whose early death meant that Oscar had never got to know him properly. His mother, a one-man woman, as she liked to call herself, had not remarried. She remained wedded to an absence that cast a long shadow both forward and back. The dream that woke him was not new: it was of his mother raising her arm like a drawbridge in an attempt to wave.

He knew where the image sprang from. "You should get me some poison, Oscar. I cannot, will not go on like this." It had not been a recommendation, rather a nonnegotiable order. The belligerence of a very old, lifelong pacifist. The words did not seem to be her own, just as her voice seemed to rise from unknown depths, dark, imperious, even repellent at times. Week after week saw her intoning her mantra of self-willed death, and him refusing to act on it. His loving, strong, desperate mother, who subsequently threatened to throw herself from the window. The ultimate deed, the rebellion of a life under duress. She meant what she said, of that he had been convinced. His response had been no less adamant: she should stop eating and drinking, he would stay with her, keep vigil, hold her hand to the last. He knew a doctor who would prescribe morphine if the pain grew unbearable. At length she conceded. When the doctor came with his potion for everlasting sleep and Oscar took her hand in his, she said: "I won't have to jump now."

The nights on a mattress beside her bed would stay with him forever. So would the groans and whimpers of her frame, now shrunken to a comma. A night on a mattress, two steps away from death, lasts a long time. The feeble wave of a stray arm, raised at a passing signal, at the moon through the clouds. So much is certain: in the hour of our vanishing all is unknown.

Chapter 16

"Kate de Winther?" a courteous voice inquired from below. Her name sounded droll in Italian, she thought. She was sitting on her balcony waiting for Roy, whom she expected any moment. She leaned over the stone balustrade. The man looking up at her wore the Italian railway uniform.

"Lost your way, have you? The station is miles away," she retorted laughingly. To her surprise, there was no reply. All he did was motion her to come down. So Kate was left to smile at her own joke as she descended the cool stairs in her bare feet. Her pale yellow dress was almost white in the sunshine, and she remembered thinking how hot the railway man must be feeling. He began to say something she did not understand. She would never understand. He must have caught her as she fell.

The scene leaping unbidden into her mind was one that had obsessed her a lifetime ago. In the days before Oscar.

She was on a different balcony now, her lookout post at the beginning and end of each day. Since Oscar turned up out of nowhere, everything that had previously been firmly in place had come loose. Her life with Roy had returned in all its intensity. "Forgetting is the enemy of happiness," she had read on a calendar somewhere, words of wisdom she had dismissed at the time, thinking you could just as well turn it around and say "Happiness is the ability to forget," and that had been her solution. But it hadn't worked. Because this deferred grief, or rather the melting of the frozenness, the exquisite act of remembrance, had been going on for days now. She no longer opposed it. Kate de Winther, that was who she was, the old name she was so comfortable with, the best of names, better even than her maiden name.

What would Roy have done if he knew about Barbarossa, she asked herself over and over, until she could think of nothing else. Then she knew. All right, she would go to Oscar's bosses, or to the Foreign Ministry, if need be to the Dutch queen herself, she would spread the news, whatever Oscar said. Somebody had to. Why oh why had she left it so late—they couldn't go on ignoring it, Oscar, that was simply unacceptable. Those poor innocent souls along the borders, they would all die. It was June 19. There was still time.

Kate caught sight of Matteous on the pavement of Barkston Gardens, coming toward her with the uncertain gait of a fugitive. She felt a pang of misgiving. It was the gait of someone who might retreat at any moment, double back, go home, in any case vanish from there.

"Matteous!" She waved. Matteous looked up, and even at that distance she was struck by the whites of his eyes. The black jacket of his uniform suited him.

"I'll be right down to let you in."

When he entered without his satchel, she knew something was wrong. She had known from the moment she saw him. He had come to say that he was leaving.

During the few seconds that he stood in her room, not knowing how to begin and what to do with his hands, it became clear to her how dearly she loved him, with a kind of love unlike what she felt for anybody else. Not the possessive kind, nothing to do with jealousy or resentment or self-pity. Matteous had dismantled all her defenses, she felt laid bare like an archaeologist's find. It was beyond comprehension.

She wanted to tell him about Operation Barbarossa, had to discuss it with him before it was too late, ask him if he thought she was right to go to the Ministry, even if her husband said it would put Emma in danger. Which was just an idea he had got in his head, because who on earth would suspect Emma? You do think I'm right, don't you Matteous?

But she forgot to ask him, she forgot it all. She heard only one thing.

"I cannot live in this city, Miss Kate. I have tried for your sake, but it's no good."

Her eyes caught on a button hanging by a thread from his jacket, a tarnished brass button, of the kind she had seen in her mother's button box.

No tears, please. Very briefly, she gripped the back of a chair. She had to pull herself together, suggest making tea, or coffee. Coffee, of course. Africans like their coffee black, with lots of sugar, he had said to her one day. Come and sit with me, Matteous, at the table where we always sit, face to face, paper and ink at hand, a copybook, two pens. Museum exhibits from the past.

"Won't you sit down?"

He complied with an air of signing his death warrant. Sat ramrod-straight, mute and motionless.

Gulls circled above the small park, their shrieks echoing in the room.

* * *

In Rome the doors to their balcony had been open practically all the time. Roy often sat there to write or read, quite undisturbed by the bustle of the Corso or the cries of Italian street folk.

"Tomorrow I'll be off to Milan for that Forum conference. Afterward, why don't we go to Capri? It's ages since we've been there, and Marina Piccola will be wonderfully quiet at this time of year. I could do with a break from all the brushing and scrubbing. And how about having a few babies?"

Said laughingly. Castles in the air. Kate had lifted the hem of her skirt and perched herself on his knee, asking in a mock-earnest tone: "Doesn't having babies give you varicose veins?"

Matteous and Roy, the dream of return, the return of the dream.

She asked Matteous when he would leave and how he would travel. He did not know. All he knew was that he would jump in front of a bus if he stayed. This time she made no attempt to persuade him otherwise, unlike in the past. She could hear his sad determination, and his concern for her.

He asked how they could stay in touch, and repeated what he had said about owing his life to her. Would she like to come to Africa one day? Torn between opposing nostalgias, already. He would not go back to being a soldier, nor would he go down the mines again. He would find a rubber plantation, perhaps. Work in the forest, far away from barracks and mine shafts. Become a rubber tapper.

Kate felt the rough sleeve of the uniform against her cheek, opened her eyes, and found herself slumped in the arms of the railway man lowering her gently to the ground. People came running, cries of *dottore, dottore!*, a neighbor rushed forward with a jug of water and a towel. She saw the distraught face of the Italian, the unwilling messenger of doom, the upright citizen doing his duty by sowing death and destruction. The brass buttons on his uniform caught her eye, as they had in a photograph in the accident dossier. Tokens of impending loss.

She faced Matteous, who noticed how pale she was.

"Shall I get you a glass of water?"

Kate shook her head, she did not need anything, all she wanted was to sit and wait for the reflux of the tide that had been washing over her for days: the hours with Roy and their great life together, which she had buried and banished, and which had started anew in the dark shape of Matteous.

Marina Piccola in May, which you could reach on foot over the newly constructed Via Krupp, a miraculous road with tier upon tier of hairpin bends seeming to spill from the cliffs. The Faraglioni rose high from the sea, three great spurs of black rock with seagulls wheeling above. Roy and she had seen them at close quarters from a dinghy. "Kate-ate-ate!" Roy shouted upward, outshouting the gulls. The sound came back again and again, louder each time.

Capri in early spring, almost empty of tourists. Roy supervised excavations, and she wandered around the island, or took a boat tour to the blue grotto. Roy needed only to thrust a stick in the soil to be transported to Antiquity. They had stayed for several weeks at a stretch. Kate knew the island like the back of her hand, from the Emperor Tiberius's Villa Jovis up to Monte Barbarossa.

She told Matteous of her fears for the impending invasion. She hid nothing, relating all Oscar's objections and describing his concerns over Emma's safety. She explained her own reservations, and that she had overcome them, and that she had decided to go to the authorities before it was too late.

Matteous shook his head. "Don't do it, Miss Kate, don't do it."

She had been so confident of his approval. He knew the meaning of war, he would tell her she should go, would accompany her even. But what he said was: "You must think of your daughter, Miss."

Perhaps she had spoken too quickly for him to understand, she would explain all over again, and would continue explaining until he finally said yes. But again he said no. No, no, she was not to go there, she was not to betray her daughter. They would find out, and there was nothing she or anybody else could do about the war, which was a massive force taking possession of the world, of limitless momentum and impossible to stop. Matteous expressed it otherwise, but that was what she understood him to say. He had seen the war and been unable to escape. There was no escape.

Of the funeral she had no memory, none at all but for one thing. Among the scores of mourners at the Cimitero degli Inglesi in Rome, she had seen her father holding hands with a little girl in a black hat. Who she was she did not know—a niece? The daughter of a friend?—yet it seemed to her that the child was leading him by the hand rather than the other way around. She saw herself standing at the graveside while the coffin was lowered, her eyes fixed on her mute father and the little girl in the hat. That was the only image that had stayed with her.

"Matteous, all those people will get shot and burned and blown to smithereens, they'll crush everything in their path with their tanks. They have done it before and they will do it again. We must give all those innocent folk some warning."

Matteous looked away, his hand on his heart. He was no longer listening. She was afraid he would leave without a further word. But he moved his hand from his heart to her arm, touched her wrist, and slipped her a folded scrap of paper.

Darkness fell slowly, the street lamps of Barkston Gardens remaining unlit. Time for blackout, time to stand up and shut the windows and the doors to the balcony. It was as though she had fallen ill. Her head was ablaze, she could feel the fever rising, her feet were as cold as ice. Time for blackout.

Chapter 17

The train to Fribourg departed on the dot. Oscar was often irritated by the never-ending quest for precision. The Swiss were maniacs, watchmakers, disciplinarians of strict regularity. Today he did not care one way or another, all he wished was for time to be abolished altogether, no clocks, no calendars, no appointments. It was Thursday, June 19, and the train departing from Berne at 9:32 a.m. would arrive in Fribourg at 10:17. By 10:28 a.m. he would be with Lara.

Oscar had asked her not to pick him up at the station, preferring to find his own way to her house in the event of him being followed. On previous occasions he had known by the time he reached Ensingerstrasse whether this was the case, but apparently today it was not. The arbitrariness of whether or not one was targeted by those sorry types was confounding. A matter of nobody being available, most likely.

Once more he found himself in the company of sleeping soldiers. Wherever he went—Portugal, England, Switzerland—there were soldiers lounging in doorways or huddled in corners fast asleep. War was tiring.

Fribourg. He had gone past it so often, without ever asking himself who lived in the medieval toy city. Now he had been there repeatedly, within a short space of time. Lara lived in the very center, near the wall tied like a ribbon around the old streets. His wish for the abolition of time appeared to have been granted in Fribourg: there was hardly any town in Europe quite so redolent of the Middle Ages.

The muffled throbbing of the wheels over the track held the cadence of reunion. He longed to see her, touch her, brush the hair from her eyes, have her hand covering his. And yet, for the first time, he also felt uneasy. A vague sense of foreboding, a gathering apprehension. She would ask him why he had gone off to London so suddenly, and he would have to give her a straight answer. He had to be straight with her now.

Down the platform, across the hall to the exit, up the steep hill to the old city, it was a matter of ten minutes. Straining at a taut leash, animated by desire.

"Oscar!"

She stood in the open window of the first floor, the sun shining on her laughing face.

Under her spell again, yet conscious of that strange sliver of desolation. Lara opened the door, out of breath from running down the stairs.

"The chamois of Fribourg! How quick you are, Lara."

He clasped her hand with both of his, and leaned over to lay his cheek against their hands in humble greeting, as though bowing before some fragile enigma. With equal solemnity, Lara placed her free hand on his nape. During the second that they stood thus, all was in dreamed-of balance. Their lives touched. It was a gesture of tranquil awaiting, the rapprochement of those who know not where they are going, what they are doing, or how to move ahead.

She led him up the stairs to her room, into her arms and into the sun streaming in through the open window; he heard the carefree sounds of the street and how they fell away, leaving only her arms and her mouth and their surrender.

Afterward, having got up from the bed, Oscar found himself standing very still by the window, reflexively on the lookout for a spy. As though there were two of him, as though his soul were moving from the one to the other as a precautionary safe haven. A Thursday morning in Switzerland, a sun-drenched hour of innocence and peace. Nothing untoward, you would think. The river flowed past, clouds sailed across the sky. He wondered what the time was, and what the date.

"Why did you need to go to London at such short notice?"

Geneva, Lausanne, Berne, Lisbon, London, Fribourg—the trajectory of a single word, whispered in confidence, then the terrifying ramifications, the biting of the tongue. Never in his life had he felt so torn. He had the ability to juggle with veracity, to don disguise and shed it at will, to roam free without leaving traces, to be the player in a casino of his own devising, but for the past weeks it was the case that Oscar Verschuur harbored a secret that was too important to keep to himself, and yet impossible to share with anybody else. He knew that hundreds of thousands of people would be butchered three days hence, before daybreak even, and he also knew that his information was worthless. It would not be credited. There was a complete lack of trust on every side, so that Emma's sacrifice would be pointless, supposing he were crazy enough to say anything.

Both Lara's hands rested gently on his wrist, as an intimate entreaty for an explanation, for the truth.

"It's Operation Barbarossa, the invasion of Russia. June 22nd, three days from now. Emma told me, that time in Geneva. She knew from Carl."

"So you relayed that to London. Thank goodness they'll be prepared, to some extent at least." Her tone was pragmatic, without a trace of naivety.

No, Lara, he had changed his mind, he had turned tail at the last moment. They would not have believed him for any number of reasons, such as that the intelligence came from a German source, which made it corrupt by definition. The exact date was meaningless, the attack would be launched anyway sooner or later. His version. His last resort, because of Emma. Everything else was ruled out by the unthinkable likelihood of Emma being charged with treason. Oscar could hear his own voice accounting for himself, using all the arguments and explanations he had learned by rote.

Lara's silence was disturbing. She had let go of his wrist, and had put her hands in the pockets of her dressing gown. Hiding the hands in that way is to hide the mind. She wished he would stop talking, wished she had not heard right. She drew herself away from him and drifted, faster and faster, out of the room, out of her house, back into the snow, to the time when there was only a village, a breathtaking view, no future, no past, no time. Away from him as he held forth, piling one excuse on top of the other in his blinding fear for his daughter. Fear corrupts. No one will know what I know, Lara, no one sees what I see: my child at the hands of the Gestapo.

Lara's shoulders said enough. The way she recoiled, between despair and outrage, between anguish and resignation. She knew that talking was not going to help, he had it all worked out, he had the whole chess game in his head, there was no way of getting through to him, not even for her. Or was there?

"Remember the Norwegian house at the Hunnenfluh?"

A voice from the light, an angel from the Berner Oberland. It sounded more like a statement than a question. What was that about, why did she mention that house? They had seen it and talked about it, a dream house, an unattainable Viking fantasy with small dragons guarding the drainpipes and brightly colored ornaments on turrets and balconies, a work of art for the benefit of lone mountaineers, who would watch in wonder as the elfin occupants flitted from one window to the next. Imagine living there, Lara, with no one to disturb us—he had said something like that to her once.

"I would have loved to go there every winter of our lives."

He had heard what she said; I *would have* loved. No anger, no stridency, no hostility there, only finality. Lara had nothing more to say. He could see their Norwegian house sliding down the hillside. The rapid ebbing of a love that was hardly underway.

Chapter 18

Emma pressed Wapenaar's doorbell a second time. In her impatience at finding every available wall covered with roses, she had dropped her bicycle on the ground. The wheel was still spinning when Wapenaar opened the door. They recognized each other immediately. He was delighted to see her, an opportunity at last to have a chat with the daughter of his good friend Verschuur. Was there anything he could do for her? Please come in, he would begin by making them a cup of coffee.

She was struck by the silence in the house. Where was his wife? The room he showed her into was a riot of coziness, with lace doilies on the tables, an upright piano, walls covered in framed watercolors and photographs of gentlefolk in nineteenth-century poses. There were lamps with pastel-colored shades, flower-filled vases, a fireplace with neatly stacked logs alongside, all of which she remarked without taking it in. She had no time to waste. She was afraid she was too late.

The days had passed in unbearable suspense and vacillation. She had not said anything to Carl. He had likewise avoided the subject. How odd not to breathe a word about what was going through your mind all day and all night. Carl Regendorf, on secondment to an organization involved in Radio Free India: broadcasts of freedom fighters in folk costumes seeking to undermine the British Raj. Their leader, a dark-skinned Indian who had shaken hands with Ribbentrop during a press conference, was in good cheer and excellent health, loudspeaker at the ready for the rant against the British oppressor. Carl had been present, fascinated by the zealotry, but above all disillusioned by the banal distortions of the truth. Over at the ministry, secret meetings were being held all the time to discuss the impending massacre and how to inveigle a way into international acquiescence. Encroaching on the edges of a redrawn map of Europe was the dawn of a new, everlasting empire. Russia, Africa, India, it would not be long now.

As long as Trott stayed put, so would he, but he was finding it increasingly difficult to stick by his resolve. The hypocrisy had assumed such proportions that he took to dropping in at Trott's office from time to time, to regale him with a mime show. Using a range of crazed grimaces and gesticulations, he imitated the antics of the regime's top dogs and ridiculed the insanity of everyday reality. Trott was highly amused by this, and communicated his responses in basic sign language, mindful of any microphones that might be concealed in lamps or ceilings. It was resistance in miniature, a scuffle in a soap bubble. But it allowed them to breathe.

In the early morning of that Thursday, as every Thursday, the bells of the nearby church rang out. Practice runs by the carilloneur, who favored a slow, penetrating rhythm. Emma loved hearing the peals that reminded her so strongly of her schooldays in Leeuwarden.

She had seen the sun slanting into her garden, she had wished her neighbor good morning when he put his hand up over the hedge, she had refreshed the date on Carl's desk calendar: June 19. Another three days to go. Then she had shaken herself awake, wheeled out her bicycle. Carl had left for work long since. She would tell Wapenaar, the secret had become too heavy to bear. It seemed less and less likely that her father had done anything, because if he had he would have found some way of letting her know. No, something must have happened to make him decide against passing on the information. Could it be something to do with that girlfriend of his? Emma's revulsion at her father's infidelity had barely abated. And it had reopened an old issue. The unforeseen separation from her father and mother, the way she had been left behind at her grandparents' home. Her father had promised that they would take her with them wherever they went, but it was a lie, he had broken his promise, and the hurt had not healed well. She was the offspring of diplomats, which made her homeless. That was how she was feeling these past days.

But Wapenaar would sound the alarm, she was certain. Telegrams would be sent all over the place via Sweden, the Russians would receive warning. It would be just in the nick of time, it had to be. The race against the clock loomed over her like an unbeatable monster of velocity. She pedaled with suppressed rage and fear, her legs and feet in constant, forceful motion. Emma covered the distance in half the time it had taken her before. The lanes she had lingered over then, fraught with indecision, now flew past. She was blind to them as she cycled past one landmark after another, turning left and right unerringly, and not reducing speed until she swerved into Wapenaar's driveway, with pounding heart but scarcely out of breath.

He placed the coffee cup in front of her, and looked at her calmly.

"Emma Verschuur, no, I should say Mrs. Regendorf, how are you? And your husband? Still at the Foreign Office?"

She nodded, came straight to the point, told him about the operation, the date, the reliability of her source: Carl.

She listened for sounds in the house that were not there. No footfalls, no creaking floorboards, no doors being opened or closed. Midges danced behind the windowpanes. Outside, the neighbors' dog started barking.

Wapenaar sat facing her. Defendant and judge, in abeyance of the verdict. Surrounding her were Carl, Watse, Trott, her father and mother, all waiting with her. Then came his questions, the most amicable cross-examination you could imagine. At last someone who would do something, take action. But there was no verdict. Wapenaar thanked her, showed her out, raised his hand as she cycled away, followed her with his eyes.

The return journey through Grunewald to Dahlem was the worst. Emma shivered as though she had a fever. The verdict, if any, was hers to reach. The alert would course through the circuit of diplomats and politicians, coded messages would be placed on the desks of ambassadors: Operation Barbarossa, June 22. Who else knew about this in Moscow, or in Berlin, or in Berne, London, Washington and Ankara? Was it true, was it all about to begin, or was it an unexploded bomb, an airman's signal high in the sky, was it Zero Hour, or perhaps not after all? The Swedes would have picked up the news somewhere, no, the Swiss, it came from a trustworthy source in Berlin. Who said that, let them come forward, we know nothing, is it a trap, a stab in the back, an act of despair?

How long before it reaches Prinz-Albrecht-Strasse, how long before her name crops up, and Carl's name—one week, two, a month perhaps?

A car was speeding along the lanes of Dahlem, with the all too familiar squeal of tires taking sharp corners. Elbows jutting nonchalantly from the windows, shiny long coats with wide belts. The siren would not be switched off when they blocked the entrance with their squad car. There would be pounding on the door as the violence burst in on their lives, never to leave.

Emma cycled home in a cloud of fantasy and conjecture, and of bitter visions.

Chapter 19

Would you switch the wireless on, Matteous?

She had no idea of the time, could be morning, could be evening. Probably evening, she thought. Kate had been in bed with a high fever for the past three days. Matteous nursed her to the best of his ability, fetching glasses of water, laying damp cloths on her forehead, standing guard by the bedroom door. Everything was turned on its head: she in bed, he beside it. Kate talked in her sleep, sounding delirious. Matteous listened to her nocturnal ramblings, and waited. When she was awake she wanted to get out of bed, but could not. She had lost all power over her arms and legs. She had become the child of Matteous, who watched over her and rocked her cradle. Gone were her will and her courage, her body abided by its own rules. There was no way she could go to a minister, or to the Queen.

Churchill's voice wafted through the room. In Kate's head everything sounded as if it came from twice as far away, but the meaning was clear. She knew what he was announcing, she had known for the past fortnight. But she had not heard it said in this way, had never grasped the full portent of it as she did now, in the terse, half-mumbled, half-sung speech by the English prime minister. He was saying the same things she had said to Carl: they would all be wiped out, all those mothers and children, and those poor ragged peasants having to fight with their bare hands against a terrible war machine, it was sheer betrayal, it was the slaughter of a people taken completely by surprise.

The German armies were massed along a line stretching from the White Sea to the Black Sea, and their armored divisions had attacked Russia. Bombs rained down upon the towns and villages, harvests were laid waste. The Nazis were after Russia's oil.

Churchill's words hammered in her head. He predicted that after Russia it would be the turn of China and India, where the lives and happiness of a thousand million human beings were now under threat. And then Kate heard him say: "I gave him warnings, I gave clear and precise warnings to Stalin of what was coming." Kate glanced at Matteous, whose face remained impassive throughout.

I gave him warnings. So Oscar had gone to the English after all. He had listened to her—thank God for that. She smiled faintly and fell asleep again.

She had fallen violently ill from one day to the next, almost as if this was her last chance to make him stay just a little longer. An alibi for Matteous to put his plans on hold until she recovered. And of course he would do that for her, he would stay until further notice. Notice from the heartlands of Africa, from a nameless rubber plantation. A call from nobody in particular, but one that was heard and understood by Matteous.

The folded note he had given her bore his plan, set out in hieroglyphics. The words had come out in an instinctive, erratic scrawl, English and French sounds buried in a script resembling barbed wire, which Kate had difficulty reading. It must have taken him days to write. His farewell letter. The sadness welling up in her became conflated with her soaring temperature. She had already been shivering, her hand already shaking, when he had slipped her the note.

He had said that he would take care of her until she was well again. Then he would leave.

The summer began splendidly on Sunday, June 22. Emma went into the garden, in answer to her private roll call. It was eight o'clock, not a sound, only birdsong. Carl was asleep. He had not come home until dawn, having worked all night at the ministry. Emma had listened quietly when he told her of the attack, a saber thrust deep in the flank of Russia. 3.8 million men had crossed the border, 150 divisions, Germans, Romanians and Finns, 2,000 aircraft, 600,000 motor vehicles, over 600,000 horses, 7,100 artillery guns, 3,350 tanks, over a distance of 1,800 miles, and all this at 03:15 hours sharp. He had read it out to her from a slip of paper.

"The gangsters."

She stood in her garden, thinking of nothing in particular. There were no bombs exploding around her, no shots being fired. No tanks, no artillery. No grenades being tossed. Where was everybody? Just then the church bells began to ring, calling the village to worship as they did every Sunday, rain or shine, war or no war. Emma waited for the noise of a car speeding up the road. Better to be prepared.

But silence prevailed, and the sun shone as never before.

Oscar looked at his watch, as he had done throughout the night, hour after hour, until it was light enough for him to go outside. Not a soul around. Ensingerstrasse was a channel of emptiness, with more emptiness around the corner. At home he had heard the long-dreaded and long-avoided news on the German radio from Goebbels, speaking on behalf of the Idiot: "German people! National Socialists! Weighed down with heavy cares, condemned to months-long silence, the hour has now come when at last I can speak frankly."

He had sat staring at the radio, and then tuned in to the B.B.C., where it was claimed that repeated warnings had been given to Stalin and the Russians. He did not believe it. Of course they hadn't given out warnings, it was the last thing they would do. What better than to have Germany fighting on two fronts? It was to Britain's advantage that Russia was now involved, and he had no doubt that Churchill was rejoicing. Would he come on the radio, Oscar wondered, and would Morton be with him?

He had not spoken again with Lara, but she was imprinted on his every movement. Returning from Fribourg he had even stood for a while across the street from the home of his Swedish colleague Henderson, thinking: if I ring the doorbell now I can give a last-minute warning, and who knows, throw a tiny wrench in the works of the Wehrmacht. He had not acted upon the thought.

Oscar wandered aimlessly on, away from the radio broadcast. The first early hikers, sturdily shod and bearing knapsacks, crossed his path.

OTTO DE KAT is the pen name of Dutch publisher, poet, novelist and critic Jan Geurt Gaarlandt. His highly acclaimed novels have been widely published in Europe, and *Man on the Move* was the winner of the Netherlands' Halewijn Literature Prize.

INA RILKE is the prize-winning translator of books by Cees Nooteboom, W. F. Hermans, Erwin Mortier, Louis Couperus, Hella Haasse and Adriaan Van Dis.

About the Type

Typeset in Albertina at 11.5/15 pt.

Albertina was created by calligrapher Chris Brand. Due to mechanical limitations of the 1960s, his original designs had to be altered drastically to conform with a uniform grid. The rise of digital typographic tools later allowed Frank E. Blokland and the Dutch Type Library to release Albertina with the original forms of Chris Brand's calligraphy-inspired forms.

Typeset by Scribe Inc., Philadelphia, PA